# THE SHOE TESTER
# OF FRANKFURT

# THE SHOE TESTER
# OF FRANKFURT

A NOVEL BY
## WILHELM GENAZINO

TRANSLATED FROM THE GERMAN
BY PHILIP BOEHM

A NEW DIRECTIONS BOOK

Originally published by Carl Hanser Verlag as *Ein Regenschirm für diesen Tag* in 2001. The German title of this novel, *Ein Regenschirm für diesen Tag*, translates literally as *An Umbrella for this Day*. The title *The Shoe Tester of Frankfurt* was chosen by the Publisher.

The publication of this work was supported by a grant from the Goethe-Institut.

Book design by Sylvia Frezzolini Severance
Manufactured in the United States of America
New Directions Books are printed on acid-free paper.
First published as a New Directions Paperbook (NDP1037) in 2006
Published simultaneously in Canada by Penguin Books Canada Limited

Library of Congress Cataloging-in-Publication Data

Genazino, Wilhelm, 1943–
[Ein Regenschirm für diesen Tag. English]
The shoe tester of Frankfurt / Wilhelm Genazino ;
translated from the German by Philip Boehm.
   p. cm.
ISBN-13: 978-0-8112-1583-1 (alk. paper)
ISBN-10: 0-8112-1583-0
I. Boehm, Philip. II. Title.
PT2667.E54R4413 2006
833'.914—dc22

                                        2006009105

New Directions Books are published for James Laughlin
by New Directions Publishing Corporation
80 Eighth Avenue, New York, NY 10011

For Barbara

# THE SHOE TESTER
# OF FRANKFURT

# 1

TWO SCHOOL CHILDREN ARE STANDING IN FRONT OF A kiosk. They spit on a poster and laugh at the spittle running down the column. I pick up my pace; I used to be a lot more tolerant of that sort of thing. I regret how easily disgusted I am these days. A few more swallows go flying through the pedestrian underpass. They swoop down into the subway station, and eight or nine seconds later come darting back out the other side. I'd like to cut through the tunnel myself and make it across just in time to feel the swallows rushing past me. But that's one mistake I'm not about to repeat. I went through that tunnel two or three weeks ago, and I'll never do it again. The swallows flitted right by me—the whole thing only lasted two or three seconds, sad to say— and that's when I discovered the wet pigeons, which I hadn't noticed at first. They were huddled together in a corner of the tiled floor. Two homeless people were sprawled on the ground trying to get their attention by making noises and waving their hands. When the birds didn't react, the homeless people started making fun of them. And right after that I noticed this dried-up spot of ketchup on the tip of my right shoe. I had no idea how it got there, and I had no idea how I'd managed to miss it earlier. That's the last time you're going through that tunnel, I said to myself, just as a joke. I can see Gunhild on the other side of the underpass. I'm a little afraid of women named Gunhild or Gerhild or Mechthild or Brunhild. Gunhild goes about her life barely perceiving anything on her own. I must be blind, she often says. She says it in jest but really means it. You have to point out what she could be seeing, then she's content. At the moment I don't feel any great need to talk to Gunhild, so I backtrack a ways up Herderstrasse to avoid meeting her. If Gunhild ever did open her eyes she might see how I run away from her, at least sometimes.

Two minutes later I'm already beginning to regret that she isn't with me. Because Gunhild has the same eyelashes as Dagmar, whom I loved back when I was sixteen, there at the outdoor swimming pool, where we lay on my mother's ironing blanket. Where most other women have just one eyelash, Dagmar had two or three or even four; in fact you could say her eyes were tufted with lashes. And Gunhild's eyes are exactly the same. When I stare at her long enough, I feel I'm right back on the ironing blanket, sitting next to Dagmar. In my mind it's not the experiences that make a person unforgettable—it's the physical details that truly strike us, long after we've parted ways. To tell the truth I really don't want to be reminded of Dagmar today, even though I've spent the past several minutes thinking about her—now I've gone so far as to remember the color of her bathing suit. Our childish love came to an unhappy end. The following year Dagmar showed up at the pool toting a pair of goggles, which she put on every time we went into the water. As a result I could no longer see her eyelash-tufts, which were especially beautiful in the sun and water that made them glisten and gleam like little grains of sugar. At the time I didn't dare tell Dagmar the reason for my backing out. Even today I feel a ridiculous little twinge when I hear myself whispering: Dagmar, it was the goggles.

Outside St. Nicholas Church, where a small circus is currently performing, a young woman asks me if I could look after her suitcase for a moment. Sure, I say, why not. I'll be back in ten minutes, the woman says. She sets the bag down next to me, gives a friendly nod and goes on her way. I'm constantly amazed that strangers are so trusting toward me. The suitcase is small and presumably well traveled. Meanwhile people are already staring at me, wondering

2

whether the suitcase and I belong to each other or not. No, we don't. I used to assume that people stared at one another because they're always afraid, wary of receiving some bad news. Then I thought their looking meant they were searching for the right words to fit life in all its peculiarity. Because their eyes are constantly atwitter with precisely that same peculiarity—though this is something that defies being looked at. These days I hardly think at all anymore; I only look around and about. And as you can see, I've taken to telling lies. Because it's impossible to wander around town without thinking. At the moment I'm thinking how nice it would be if people were suddenly poor again. And I mean everybody, all at once. How nice it would be if I could see them without their sunglasses, handbags, crash helmets, racing bikes, pedigreed dogs, rollerblades, atomic watches— with nothing on but the same rags they'd been wearing for years. At least for half an hour.

Just now I'm a little out of sorts; I can't figure out why. Since early this morning I've felt a deep and thorough understanding for every form of poverty. Two stinking men come walking past me and I just put up with them without a moment's hesitation. They're homeless and bathless and they've lost their sensitivity in the bargain. You simply have to accept their poverty the way poverty has always been accepted. It's very nice to stand here with no idea who owns the suitcase you're looking after. At the edge of the circus, a young woman leads a horse off to the side and begins to groom it, running the brush over the animal's back with firm, clear strokes. Her face is close to the horse's coat. The animal lifts a leg and stamps its hoof on the pavement, producing a pleasant sort of clang. At about the same time, the horse's penis slowly extends. A few people some ways off stop to look. At first it's not clear what they're watching, but I can tell from the way two of the men are snickering that they're not so much watching as waiting for the moment

3

when the woman discovers the horse's penis. Why doesn't she just step back and take a random glance at his underbelly? The woman has no idea she has a small audience eagerly awaiting a spectacle. Oblivious, she keeps her face near the animal's back. Now! A small step off to the side is all it would take, and the show would begin.

The woman whose suitcase I'm tending comes back, carrying a prescription in her left hand. Now everything is clear: she went to the doctor's and didn't want to be seen there with a suitcase. My guess is she's not a traveler but a kind of houseless urban nomad. She thanks me and takes back her suitcase. I'd like to warn her not to be so trusting, but right away I have to laugh at my own concern. The audience won't get their spectacle: the horse's penis retracts again, slowly, into its velvety sheath. My incessant looking around and about gets me into various adventures I don't particularly want, though they resemble the ones I often miss. The secret titillation among the onlookers fades away. One of the men walks up to a colorful box with the inscription: "PUT YOUR WINNING TICKET HERE!" The man shoves a small coupon through the slot. He looks back at the horse and feels compelled to laugh at how quickly the animal's erection faded. I happen to catch sight of the trainer as she nudges her face close to the animal's body. She looks as if she were on the verge of sniffing the horse's coat. Now she raises both arms and drapes them gently over the animal's back. She buries her face in the horse's flank and keeps it there for nearly three seconds. The animal stays still, peering this way and that, as always. I'm convinced that smelling the coat is a special pleasure. While all this is happening, Gunhild comes ambling across the square. She notices me and heads straight over. A sure sign that she hadn't seen or heard or thought anything since I last saw her. And that's exactly the way it is. I've been toying again with the idea that something special ought to happen to me, she says. But nothing happens! Of course I don't really want anything to happen to me, but I keep imagining it. My own personal private craziness. Why personal private? I ask. Because it isn't public and because I can control it, says Gunhild. She gradually calms down. I wonder whether I should tell her about the business with the horse and the trainer. Gunhild casts her eyes down so that I get a good look at her eyelash-tufts. Poor Dagmar! Presumably I wouldn't have much interest in Gunhild if she didn't have these particular lashes. Tomorrow or the next day I'll come back and check if the trainer is brushing down her horse again. Gunhild is standing next to me. Presumably she's waiting for me to point something out to her. The trainer leads the horse back into the stall.

You want to go to the circus? Gunhild asks, then laughs, as if to mock her own question.

Why not, I say.

You mean you'd really go to the circus? Gunhild exclaims.

Of course, I say, wouldn't you?

If I did I'd spend the whole time thinking about how I couldn't think of anything better to do than go to the circus, says Gunhild.

I have nothing to say to that, so I look at a baby right beside us slumbering away in his stroller. Whenever he hears an unfamiliar sound the baby twitches his lips in his sleep. Why the lips, why not the fingers? Since I'm annoyed at Gunhild I keep the question to myself. The mother fishes a pacifier out of her purse and shoves it into her child's mouth. As she's doing this, a number of cotton swabs drop out of her purse. They fall on the ground, spreading out at the mother's feet, all but two, that is, which land right in front of Gunhild's shoes. Oh, says Gunhild. The mother gathers up all the swabs except for the two in front of Gunhild's shoes. Gunhild could pick them both up and hand them to the mother. But Gunhild is incapable of going to the circus and she's incapable of picking up cotton swabs. In such situations all she can do is make a quick getaway. That's basically why I like her. But she always manages to disappear before I can confess this to her. Even now she's whispering a quiet *See you later!* and extracting herself from the situation. I watch her walk away until I notice a woman who's dropped a piece of gum out of her backpack. The woman is engrossed by a jeweler's window display, she didn't notice her loss. Shall I go to her and tell her: You've dropped a stick of gum? Maybe it would be enough to say: I think something fell out of your backpack. Or simply: You dropped something. To clarify things (and because I don't like saying the words *chewing gum*), I could point my index finger at the object on the ground. Except for the fact that pointing my index finger would (does) embarrass me. It's awful, I'm like Gunhild, I can't call anyone's attention to anything. Presumably the woman doesn't even want anyone to tell her about her loss. She's all dressed up in black faux leather, which makes me think she's a biker. She walks on; the chewing gum stays. As she walks, the leather makes a quiet but clearly audible squishing sound. It's an odd thing, but this squishing convinces me it was a good thing I kept my mouth shut. Besides, these days most people probably assume they're going to lose a stick of chewing gum every now and then, except once again I was too slow to realize it. All the biker woman is really interested in are the shop windows. Now she's standing outside a bakery looking at the display of nut croissants, streusel cake, and puff pastries. She steps inside and buys a pretzel. I can see her starting to eat it inside the store. Still chewing away, she steps back out onto the street and stops in front of a hair salon's display. She doesn't look at apartment buildings, entranceways, buzzer panels, doors, mailboxes, or windows. Buildings and people often have the same effect on me. You spend years—in many cases even decades—looking at people, and they look at you.

But one day certain buildings have suddenly disappeared or else they've been remodeled to such an extent that I no longer recognize many of them and then I'm so annoyed that I no longer look at them. I don't know if today is one of those days—probably not. If it were, then I'd once again have this sensation that people like me should be told to either disappear or else get remodeled like the old buildings. This sensation is connected with another feeling I often have, namely that I'm here in this world without my inner authorization. Strictly speaking I'm still waiting for someone to ask me whether I really *want* to be here. I imagine how nice it would be if I could grant myself this permission, let's say this afternoon. As for the question of *who* should ask me to grant this permission, I have no idea—but that doesn't matter.

Apart from the biker I see a paramedic dressed in a white-and-red plastic jacket, and a security guard, wearing a trim and tidy uniform, standing beside the entrance to a bank. He eyes the passersby as though they radiated danger. Both the paramedic and the guard look like individuals whose value has recently declined quite a bit. If someone were to show up and want to buy the paramedic, for example, I don't think he'd have to pay more than five marks. The biker wouldn't cost much, either; nor, incidentally, would I, because of the missing authorization. A boy of about twelve is sitting down on the rim of the city fountain. He has a small sailboat that he carefully lowers into the water. The jets are set low today, so the surface of the water is barely moving. Soon a light wind fills both of the ship's sails and drives it slowly across the basin. I take a seat on the rim of the fountain near where the boat is likely to arrive. It shouldn't need more than a few minutes to make the crossing, assuming it manages to sail by the jets unscathed and the wind doesn't slacken. Without taking his eyes off the boat, the boy walks slowly around the fountain, completely ignoring the young women who are also perched on the edge of the fountain, chatting away. Nor do the women take any interest in the boy. I watch the boat like someone who has a lot invested in its arrival. The wind carries isolated words from the women over to me. At night... the woman on the left is saying, at night... I often ask myself... when I can't sleep... After that I can't make out any more. The little sailboat is just now landing on my side of the fountain. The boy reaches into the water, joyfully retrieves his ship, and carries it off under his arm like a living animal he will never surrender.

Susanne Bleuler comes bounding out of Grenadier Strasse. I hope she doesn't see me. I've known her since we were children, and to this day hardly a week goes by that we don't bump into each other. I don't know what to say to her now and it's been ages since I did. Whatever might have been between us once upon a time crumbled into a hundred wavering indecisions. Today Susanne Bleuler works as a receptionist in a large law firm. It isn't a job she likes, but she can't find anything better. In reality, Susanne considers herself an actress; she'd still prefer to be called Margarita Mendoza. When she was young she actually did attend an acting school and afterward was hired on at two or three small theaters. That was about twenty-five years ago. I've never seen her on any stage myself. Which is why I can't judge whether she is or was a good, bad, mediocre or ill-starred actress. I'm not allowed to call her Margarita Mendoza because the name reminds her of her failed career. But I can't call her Susanne Bleuler either, since her real name reminds her of the naïve wishes of her childhood. Actually it's more complicated than that. In her inner self, I fear, she considers her failure to be unjust. She refers to "theater circles" with the greatest disdain, as if there were a lot of people who remember her as an actress and who yearn to see her back on stage. Now she's moving on, heading straight for the law firm, I suppose. She hardly looks up; I imagine she's repeating lines to herself, forgetting that she no longer needs them. Up in the sky I notice a glider. Silent, white and slow it glides away, forming huge circles in the blue of the firmament. In me Susanne Bleuler has someone who can vouch for the authenticity of her desires, because when she was only twelve she confessed to me during a sled ride—I was sitting behind her on a two-seat toboggan—that she was going to be an actress and nothing else. That was the first time I'd ever touched a girl's breasts. For a long time I didn't realize I was dealing with a bosom. I always simply sat in back of Susanne and held onto her from behind. Nor did she notice that both of my hands were on top of her breasts every time. It wasn't until she turned thirteen that she suddenly shoved my hands aside and laughed. I laughed too, and that shared laughter was the first time we realized that there were breasts and hands and something new and scary between us that quickly drove us apart, at least for a while.

To this day Susanne wants to talk to me about these details, which she calls the details of our unique childhood. For example, she finds it interesting that I always sat behind her on the toboggan. If I had sat in front I wouldn't have been able to touch her bosom. Only the back seat gave me the opportunity to do that. So even then I obviously had reason to stick to that particular seating order come what may. No matter how many times I tell her I couldn't possibly have felt that she even had a bosom under her parka, her sweater, her blouse, and her undershirt, Susanne still refuses to believe me. By the same token I no longer like talking about my childhood. The only reason I end up wandering around and about the city so much is that it makes it easier for me not to remember. Nor would I want to have to explain why I no longer like to remember my childhood. And I certainly wouldn't want to ask other people to stop speaking about my childhood. I wouldn't want my childhood to become more and more a tale about my childhood, I'd prefer to preserve it as something lingering behind my eyes—moody, muddled, biting. Susanne on the other hand believes that speaking about one's childhood gives rise to a new, second childhood—which in my opinion is utter nonsense. Back then we had an argument, first in a pub, then on the street, and for the first time I considered pinning a small label to my lapel that might read: PLEASE NO CONVERSATIONS ABOUT YOUR CHILDHOOD OR MINE. Or even a tad more curtly: PLEASE AVOID THE SUBJECT OF CHILDHOOD. Of course I'd be exposing myself to all sorts of dangers and misunderstandings if I were to run around wearing a pin like that. Susanne wouldn't understand and would announce: Now you've finally lost it. She's said this quite often; she says it all the time when she doesn't understand something right away or is reluctant to accept it. I look up into the blue sky and discover a second glider. *One* glider in the sky is a miracle; *two* gliders are a public display of largesse. Now I've gone and criticized society once again! I always want to hold back but then I lose my sense of control and have a relapse. It seems that Susanne is no longer around. Otherwise she would have long since sat down next to me on the rim of the fountain, to talk about my childhood or else about Sartre's *No Exit*, in which she once played Estelle, albeit twenty-seven years ago.

I feel a pleasant tiredness pouring into me or maybe through me—I can't say which. If I could I'd lie down right here and sleep for half an hour, right next to the sparkling water. But I can't fall asleep unless I'm in an enclosed space. I get up and angle across the small square. It's noon; when they're half empty like this, the department stores are almost pleasant—quiet and meaningless. If I remember right they sell men's socks on the third floor. I roam around the ground level looking for the escalator. To my left are long shelves with shaving soap, hair tonic, tubes of shaving lotion, men's cologne, cotton swabs, skin cream, baby items. I make a small detour and turn down an aisle with household cleaners, insect sprays, and dust rags. Some ten seconds later I cause a small pack of razor blades to disappear into my jacket pocket—I can't say why. Presumably because of my disgruntlement at living without inner authorization. This department store is precisely the kind of place where I would appreciate being asked whether I really want to be in this world. I only need one pair of socks, but I'll have to walk past hundreds and personally pick up at least a dozen before I find one that suits me. Nevertheless, no one approaches me; no one takes me aside; no one asks whether I ever consented to wander about like this. Instead, I see a disabled woman moving through the aisles in her wheelchair. At the moment she's gliding past gigantic packs of toilet paper and equally gigantic packs of disposable diapers. Her small hands expertly grasp the spokes of each wheel. The sight of her makes me want to pay for the razor blades in my jacket pocket. I don't understand the connection. Evidently the appearance of someone even worse off than myself brings out the well-behaved person in me. That sounds plausible enough; in reality, however, that statement explains nothing and leaves me completely baffled. I just watch the disabled lady roll away, faster and faster, and in case someone should happen to ask, I would presumably refuse to authorize my being in the world. Now I'm already in line at the nearest checkout counter, having inconspicuously retrieved the razor blades from my jacket pocket. It looks as though I'd always intended to take them to the counter, as if such an act of rebellion against unauthorized life—no matter how veiled—were completely foreign to me. And while I'm standing in the long line, slowly inching ahead, I glance over the tops of several shelves with different wares and see the weathered face of my former friend Himmelsbach. It's been at least half a year since I last saw or spoke to him. We had a falling-out over something about seven years ago. Even then Himmelsbach wasn't doing so well; he asked if I could lend him five hundred marks. I gave him the money, but to this day he hasn't given it back. And so an old friendship went to pieces, or rather it dissolved into a series of awkward situations, one of which is starting to unfold right this minute. Years ago Himmelsbach used to work as a photographer in Paris. That is, he wanted to work as a photographer in Paris; he even rented a small apartment in the 8$^{th}$ Arrondissement, which he once let me use for fourteen days while he was traveling in the south of France. The apartment had a small kitchen, a small bathroom, and two rooms—one larger, one smaller. I wasn't allowed to use the large room; it was his private space and he locked it up while he was away. The very first day I was alone in the apartment, I noticed it was raining into the small room where I was supposed to be staying. In addition, a large chunk was missing from the windowpane, which meant the wind kept blowing in and the room was almost always cold. Because of that I stayed out for most of the fourteen days and only used the apartment for sleeping. When Himmelsbach came back, he opened the big room designated as his private space: it was perfectly dry and had a working heater to boot.

I understood; I was supposed to keep mum about the fact that it had rained into the smaller room and that the window leaked and that the space was generally uninhabitable. I left the next day, shortly after lending Himmelsbach five hundred marks. You see, his life as a photographer in Paris wasn't working out for him. Not that he wasn't photographing: he took pictures every day, but he had a very hard time selling them to newspapers and journals. There are far too many photographers in Paris, he cursed. Then he looked at me and I said: God knows there really are far too many photographers in Paris. My answer was harsher than I

12

first realized. Because it contained the possibility that Himmelsbach himself was one of the far too many photographers. Shortly after that Himmelsbach told me that the only reason he'd invited me to his apartment was because he was afraid someone might break in while he was away. I presume he's since given up photography. In any case he no longer carries his camera around with him. Once again, just like with Susanne, I hope to go unnoticed. I'm still annoyed at the woman in the wheelchair, even though she's long gone: if I hadn't caught sight of her I'd be gone by now, too. Himmelsbach is so absorbed with himself that he doesn't notice what's going on around him. His shoes are hard and gray; he probably doesn't polish them any more. He strolls around the perfume department spraying little samples from the test bottles, first on the inside of his hands and wrists and then on his arms. Every spritz makes a *pfft*. My God, I think, so that's what Himmelsbach has turned into—the kind of man who perfumes himself for free in department stores. What's more, he probably considers himself sophisticated on top of that. I can see he's turned into an elderly ghost, a *pfft*-man who will never settle his debts. Nonetheless, I manage to take the severity out of my eyes, at least for a second. If Himmelsbach were to glance my way right now he'd think I had mellowed. And then we just might be able to talk to each other despite the rained-in room and the debt, and so triumph over the awkward twists and turns of fate. But such a moment never comes. Himmelsbach can't stop picking up one tester after the other; now he's even spraying his shirt. He doesn't see that the salesgirls are already giggling at him. I ought to intervene, protect him, but I can't. Because deep inside I, too, am making fun of him, I notice how happy I am to lose sight of him, as I mutter to myself: *pfft, pfft, pfft*.

# 2

IN THE WAKE OF THESE EXPERIENCES I HAVE DECIDED NOT to buy a pair of socks today. My unplanned purchase of the razor blades was enough excitement. There's no rush with the socks; I don't need them today and won't need them tomorrow or necessarily the day after that. Besides, then I'll have an excuse to get out of my apartment again and go into town. Because apart from my strategy of not recalling my childhood while I'm walking about, there is another, much more compelling reason to avoid my apartment as often as I can, for hours at a time if possible. Admittedly I can't talk about this reason at the moment, nor can I think it over or even through. But clearly these unmentionable things are tied to the fact that I've just remembered an old death fantasy—right now, shortly after leaving the department store—which I thought I had forgotten. About fifteen years ago I had this idea that when I die I ought to be flanked by two half-naked women, who would sit close enough to my deathbed that I could easily reach out and touch their bared breasts. At the time I imagined that such physical solace would make it easier for me to cope with the impertinence of death. Hardly a day went by that I didn't wonder which of my female friends I ought to approach, just to be on the safe side, and ask if they would be prepared to perform this end-of-life service when the time came. I remember thinking it would be best to start with Margot and Elisabeth, since—how shall I put it—even when love was at its zenith, each of these women possessed the ability to soothe me in a way that demanded no action on their part. I merely had to look at them and, on occasion, touch them. I'm standing at a streetcar stop, waiting for the Number 11, which (presumably) I won't be taking home after all. All around me are waiting people—young women, older women, and a few men. The women wear light blouses that flutter or rather sway in the wind. It strikes me that women today no longer wear blouses with the cut in the front, but rather off to the side. As a result, what used to be the neckline has migrated to underneath the arms. As far as I'm concerned, breasts viewed from the side look a lot more maternal than ones viewed straight on. Presumably viewing breasts from the side will make it easier for me to cope with the fact that breasts are moving further and further out of my life and will one day disappear altogether. I wonder why I gave up on the idea of the deathbed bosom, I mean the bosom deathbed, no, I mean why I gave up on the idea of touching a bosom when I die. The longer this recollection lingers in my thoughts, the more it appeals to me. I don't know whether I asked Susanne back then or not. Right now I'm busy coming up with reasons why it makes more sense for me to forgo the streetcar. I'm so caught up with the past and future questions of my life that it seems silly to try and lug them on board a cramped and crowded streetcar. I can't do anything aboard a streetcar except ride the streetcar. Actually I have to take care not to bump into some retired person or collapse onto a lady already in her seat. Here comes the Number 11, the doors open automatically, the women reach for their shopping bags. I watch as all these people, who otherwise show no real talent for conquest, rush into the streetcar with the intent of conquering a seat. I stay outside; the streetcar pulls away. I'll cover the four or five stops on foot. To my right is Schmoller & Co., a large car dealership. Every Friday around noon they clean the big showrooms and sales offices. A young man and a young woman, presumably a married couple, drag huge canister vacuums behind them. You can hear the noise these two vacuum cleaners make from the street. I stop in front of one of the windows and act as if I were interested in new cars. In reality I'm looking at the child the two cleaning people always bring along. A girl about seven years old, who stands there among the cars looking around for her mother, so close and yet unreachable. A mother who is vacuuming is as absent as death. The mother keeps shoving the brushy nozzle underneath the cars, thereby avoiding any contact with her child. She probably loves her vacuum cleaner, since it does a tremendous job of making her inaccessible. The mother is the vacuum cleaner and the vacuum cleaner is the mother. Nor does she cross paths with her husband, but he's long since grown accustomed to the fact that both of them have turned into vacuum cleaners. There you have it! I'm quite the vacuum cleaner critic, aren't I? Just now the girl notices that there's a man standing outside and looking in. She comes right up to the glass and stares at me. This is when I ought to have the courage to ask the cleaning couple if I can take the child for a half-hour walk. They'll probably be so overjoyed that they'll give her to me. Unfortunately the thought makes me chuckle for just a second, which the girl misinterprets. She, too, laughs, and presses her forehead against the windowpane. This is the EXACT moment for me to stroll into the showroom and take the child for a walk. Instead, my watchband starts to itch. I'm used to wearing a watchband—I've been doing it for twenty-five years—except really I'm not used to it. I undo the band and cause my watch to disappear into my jacket pocket. The girl immediately recognizes the vanishing watch as a sign that nothing is going to happen. She breaks away from the windowpane and goes back to looking for her mother, who is vacuuming between two enormous SUVs. But there's the vacuum cleaner hose, snaking out from behind a radiator. Grateful to see the familiar tube being jerked along, the girl feels once more at home.

For my part I'm helped by the sight of a small pet shop

only one streetcar stop away. Or rather it's the owner of the pet shop, a man between thirty and thirty-five years old, who as usual is sitting on the steps outside his store, reading a pulp novel—whereas he should be attending to the birdcages and terrariums, which are in urgent need of cleaning. The display window needs looking after, too—immediately if not sooner. But if he cleaned the window then everyone would see the mess inside. I pause in front of the dirty glass and try to look into the store. This is meant as an act of provocation, but really it's just silly. Through the open door I once again hear the little noises the birds make as their tiny feathered bodies take off with a dense and compact flutter. Suddenly I sense that I'm going to have to pay somehow for taking so long to get home today. I shall now proceed quickly and purposefully to my apartment. Today is Friday, and every Friday an elderly woman hangs out her husband's freshly washed work shirts on their balcony. I can see the balcony from my kitchen. She always carries a plastic tub with four or five deep blue, dripping wet shirts, which she carefully hangs out to dry. After a short while the woman herself is barely visible anymore. At most I might happen to see her white arms reaching among the blue backs of the shirts. Just like the cleaning people and the pet shop owner, the workman's wife doesn't pay any attention to her surroundings. Although it will be some time before I actually see the wet shirts in front of me, the idea of seeing them sets me at ease. I cross the street and accidentally run into Doris. Right away I'm convinced that she is the punishment for all my dawdling. Doris acts as if she hasn't seen me in a long time; as always she takes care not to move too quickly. When she was little she had to be flown to America for a rare and difficult heart operation. The operation left her with a long scar that she once showed me. To this day Doris is not supposed to get too excited, since that could mean putting a dangerous strain on her heart.

You were looking inside the pet shop again, weren't you?

Were you watching me? I ask back.

Yes.

So why are you asking?

Just to ask, she says. And once again you were wondering whether you shouldn't finally buy two mice.

Doris giggles.

Me? is all I ask.

I think it's so cute that I know a man who's thinking of buying two white mice! I was just telling one of the girls at work! And imagine: she even wants to meet you, all because of the white mice!

What makes you think I want to buy two white mice!

You told me yourself.

Never in my life, I say.

But you did, says Doris, I remember perfectly.

What am I supposed to do with a couple of mice?

Don't ask me, says Doris. But that's what you said, I swear.

You must be confused.

Hardly, says Doris.

I once told you I wanted two mice *when I was a child.*

Precisely.

What do you mean precisely?

That's precisely what you told me, that you wanted two mice when you were a child.

Precisely.

You see.

But there's a difference.

A difference? What kind of difference?

There's a difference between saying you would have liked to have two mice as a child, and saying you would like to have two mice now, as an adult.

Hmmm, says Doris.

What do you mean, Hmmm?

I don't believe in those kinds of differences.

You don't have to believe in differences, I say, they just are. Differences are something you can observe. Understand? No.

It's not a matter of what you believe, in this case all that matters is what I told you, and all I told you was that when I was a child I would have liked to have white mice, you see the difference—as a child.

OK, OK, says Doris, all right, I understand, but I don't believe it. In my opinion people never forget what they wanted as children.

You're getting things mixed up again, and once more you don't realize it. I didn't say that I had forgotten what I wanted as a child.

OK, says Doris, let me finish, I meant to say that as adults we can't ever stop wishing for the fulfillment of our childhood wishes be fulfilled—no, now I've stumbled on my own words, never mind, you know what I'm trying to tell you.

Yes, I know what you're trying to tell me, but you're on the wrong track.

I know you only think that because you're ashamed.

Me? Why should I be ashamed?

You don't want to admit that you still want to have two white mice.

But Doris! If I really wanted two white mice I wouldn't hesitate to buy them, believe me!

So why do you stand there so often in front of the pet shop looking through the window? Can you explain that to me?

You'd never understand, you don't even understand much simpler matters! How do you expect to grasp something as complex as the fact that someone might stand in front of a pet shop window without any wishes or intents and that he might even do so repeatedly! There could be a hundred different reasons for doing this, but your mousy little brain can't envisage such a range of possibilities!

Right away I wish I could take back that last sentence. On the other hand, I couldn't exactly do without it. How sorry I am for having once confessed to Doris a couple of my childhood wishes, how I regret having ever told certain persons anything at all about my childhood. If I'm not mistaken, Doris is completely flabbergasted. She didn't think I was capable of being so mean. On the other hand, I wouldn't mind if I never had to have another conversation with Doris. If she walks past me with her chin in the air from now on, I can handle it. But I'm wrong. She simply snorts and says: My God what an odd bird you have become! Then she takes my arm and laughs. And on top of that she says: The thinker and the little white mice! And laughs again. Now *I'm* the one who's flabbergasted, *I'm* the one who can't think of anything else to say. At the same time I hope her heart won't be too affected by her laughing. I wouldn't want it to be my fault if her heart pumped too much or too little blood and she should suddenly collapse. I ought to turn away from her right there and walk off without a word, but I stay, since I'm the only one who knows what's wrong with Doris, in case she has a fainting spell and collapses in my arms. But Doris doesn't collapse. She looks at me with bemused eyes like an experienced mother enjoying her child's spontaneous convolutions and contortions. There's my streetcar! she suddenly blurts out and runs off. See you! she calls to me. See you! I shout back and stand there because I believe that in such situations it's polite to stand and watch as the streetcar pulls up and stops and Doris climbs in.

The truth is that you can never get rid of anyone you've ever told about your childhood. That makes me think that the message on the label I'm thinking of pinning to my lapel really ought to be a little clearer. Maybe something like: PLEASE REFRAIN FROM SPEAKING ABOUT CHILDHOOD IN MY PRESENCE. Or else: WARNING! IF YOU SPEAK ABOUT YOUR CHILDHOOD OR MINE, THEN—no, that's too brusque. It's best if I stick with my original wording. But I can't remember what it was. My God, I don't remember the phrase I wanted to use to protect myself against the distortions of my childhood. Doris is sitting in the streetcar and waving at me. The fault is entirely my own. In recent years I have spoken too much and too indiscriminately about my childhood. I ought to stop speaking about it entirely, but presumably I won't be able to do that. I'd like to know why Doris is waving at me so persistently. As if she saw in me a truly lovable person. Either she didn't notice how malicious my last sentence was or else my wording just fell flat.

# 3

THE FIRST THING I DO WHEN I GET HOME IS GO INTO MY bedroom and sit down on the edge of the bed close to the window. From here I have a very good view of the workman's wife's balcony. I made it home just in time. Three wet shirts are already hanging on the line. Two strong white female arms come pushing between two wet shirt backs and unfold a further wet clump of material. It's the fourth deep blue shirt, which she likewise fastens to the clothesline with two plastic clothespins. I think what I admire about this work is the ambiguity; at some moments it seems utterly dull, at others, thoroughly delightful. This happens when the woman is completely given over to the shirts, just as the trainer at the circus was given over to her horse's coat. Unfortunately, however, my next move is a mistake. I take off my pants, shoes, and socks. Whenever I look at my naked feet, they're about fifteen years older than the rest of me. I study the veins that stick out so prominently, the ankles swollen like cushions, and the toenails that are growing harder and harder and taking on that sulfurous yellow color characteristic of the no longer very young. No longer very young! The only reason this euphemism is running through my head is that I have to soften the shock of my toenails. I look over at the workman's wife, but she's already gone. I'm so deeply shocked that I wander about the room in a vague and confused way and open the door to the armoire. I enjoy walking barefoot on the carpeted floor, but I don't dare look at my toenails. Opening the armoire was another mistake. Just two months ago I wasn't making mistakes like that. Until about eight weeks ago, that's where Lisa's clothes used to hang. Now it's practically empty. I remember how I used to lie on the bed and watch Lisa take a dress or a blouse out of the armoire and try it on and then ask a little later if I still found her attractive. Usually I just laughed, because I considered that the most unnecessary question imaginable. For the past two months, lying around in bed has become problematic for me. Lisa no longer lives here; Lisa left me. As long as Lisa lived here, coming home for me was the fulfillment of the good will towards men promised on earth. And I had waited half a life for this good will, ever since I first heard about it in a children's church service. But now the good will is gone. I inadvertently glance at my naked feet and sense the propaganda of abandonment they project. It used to be that I could stop being so suspicious of my life the minute I entered my apartment. Now that seems gone forever. Nevertheless, I still think it's possible that Lisa has only left me temporarily, to spur me to finally improve my "foundation." That's her way of talking about my insufficient financial grounding, which I, too, bemoan often enough these days, if more and more seldom. For the most part I no longer have the strength to look this complicated problem squarely in the eye. Meaning that I no longer understand its complex genesis, and consequently often fail to recognize what it has led to, although I myself am exactly that result. At the moment I'm thinking about the child running around the Schmoller car dealership. This lack of enthusiasm in addressing my own problems is typical for me. I realize that I'm not really thinking about the child at the car dealership. The child is simply a pupal memory of myself. I immediately recall the time I tried to kiss my mother's mouth through a veil. My mother was wearing a flat dark blue hat with a narrow brim concealing a rolled-up mesh she liked to pull down over her face. The close-lying veil made her lips and cheeks seem a little flat, as well as the tip of her nose. Presumably it was because of these minor disfigurements that I suddenly lost all desire to kiss my mother. But I kissed her anyway, and instead of my mother's skin I distinctly felt her face enmeshed in the net. For a moment the wrapped-up feeling of her lips rubbed off on my own lips. At first I enjoyed this, and kissed her just to make my own skin feel netted. No, that's not true. It was the opposite. I kept drifting further away from my mother, who was offering more and more mesh and less of her mouth. I suspected that she was deliberately rejecting her family's affection. Because I'd already noticed that my father and brother couldn't get past the net kisses any more than I could. No, that wasn't true either. The truth is, I no longer remember what really happened. My lack of clarity on this point makes me curse myself a little. It won't be much longer, I think, before they take you to a liars' asylum. Because the truth behind the truth is that naturally I think I know exactly what transpired and what did not. I have an interest in various versions of the truth, because I place value on appearing a little confused, even to myself. But the truth behind this truth is that I really can't bear to accept my own confusion and then I end up considering it really true after all. I'm amused that I coined the phrase "liars' asylum," though presumably I ought to be more alarmed. Today I see this sudden collision of memory loss and confusion or perhaps even insanity as the first indication that some disease may be spreading deep inside me. Presumably that's the only reason I'm looking to connect with some small practical activity. I enter the bathroom and brush my teeth for the second time today. In the process I look at the two dusty perfume flasks Lisa left behind. Both little bottles have been standing for years on the glass shelf under the medicine cabinet. Lisa practically never used perfume. She never tried to attract me by any artificial means. Our last attempt at intercourse slipped past us in a bizarre way. We lay next to each other for a while, with my face between her breasts, and we liked that so much that we soon fell asleep. It was as if we had both suddenly received permission to forget that there was such a thing as sexuality. When we woke up we lay linked together like an elderly married couple. With Lisa there was no need for me to grant myself an ex post facto authorization for life.

I probably ought to give Lisa a call and ask if she's planning to pick up the two perfume bottles. Or whether she forgot them—perhaps somewhat intentionally, as relics of consolation for me to look at every day. That would give me the opportunity to coolly inquire when she's coming back. I know her current phone number. She's living with her best friend Renate, at least for the time being, until she finds a new place of her own. Renate is a teacher too, just like Lisa. That is, Lisa was a teacher until about four years ago. Lisa's professional life was scarcely more than a slow initiation into its own demise. Lisa didn't want to accept the fact that she couldn't deal with the belligerent children of today. She thought she could mold her beating, biting, scratching pupils into human beings after her own image. What a mistake! After twelve years, a creeping nervous breakdown forced her to give up her profession. At first she was excused from work, then put on leave, and later forced into early retirement. Now Lisa is forty-two years old and receives a pension for having ruined herself in the name of her ideals, the state, the children, or even her illusions. Presumably Renate, who is much more flexible, won't suffer a similar fate, or if she does it will be at an appropriately later stage. I don't like the fact that Lisa is living with her. Renate is nosy and Lisa will invariably reveal the occasional intimate detail, simply out of gratitude for Renate's letting her stay there. Lisa herself won't want to, but she'll think she has no choice. Lisa's portrayals will lead Renate to think that my life, too, is a failure, and not just Lisa's. That in turn will cause me to avoid speaking with Renate altogether. And my avoiding her will only confirm Renate's conviction that I have failed. On the other hand, I don't want this idea to become fixed in Renate's mind.

Consequently I'll go out of my way *not* to avoid her, much as I would like to. I hear sobbing in the apartment, but it's only the hot water heater hiccuping. Nonetheless, I wander around the apartment looking for Lisa. I know she isn't here, I know it's idiotic of me to look for her. At times Lisa cried over me out of desperation, particularly after she had washed her hair. She would sit there, one towel wrapped around her head, another pressed against her face, a third draped over her shoulders, and sob. I would sit next to her, occasionally holding her hand, which she liked, mostly trying to figure out if there was a connection between her crying and her hairwashing. I don't wash my hair nearly as often—maybe that's why I hardly ever cry. But now it's hair-raising sentences like that that make me wonder if it's possible I'm no longer really alive in the afternoon. In reality I'm only alive in the morning, when I'm walking around and earning a little money—which I'll be doing again in the next few days. Come afternoon I experience a kind of crumbling apart, a fraying or unraveling, that I am helpless to prevent. Then I lose sight of the fact that life is made up of major as well as minor matters, since some minor matter or other grabs hold of me and won't let go. That's exactly what's happening now. From deep in the back courtyard I hear the sound of water shooting into a watering can. The watering can belongs to Frau Hebestreit, who runs a lottery booth on Teuergarten Strasse. Right about this time of day—around noon—Frau Hebestreit closes shop and waters her tomatoes, her cucumbers, and her radishes. I open the window in my kitchen that looks out onto the courtyard and sit down in the small rattan armchair beside the radiator. From there I can even hear the strange papery sound of the stream of water hitting the dusty leaves. Every day around noon, Frau Hebestreit pours five or six full cans of water onto her plants, then goes back inside her ground-floor apartment. The strong aqueous connection between the hiccups in the heater, Lisa's tears, and the water in the watering can makes me feel a considerable surge of emotion. I myself don't have to cry; the tears just well up on the inside for a moment and then disappear. Almost every day, up through the middle of May, Lisa would declare that it was still too cold. Even when we slept together in the summer she would complain about the cold. She refused to take off her nightgown; she would simply pull it up to her neck, since she wanted to be protected against a sudden case of goose pimples, for example. I would sometimes laugh silently at the sight of her nightgown bulging around her shoulders like a misshapen ruff. Once I experimented by laughing out loud, briefly (and quietly) during intercourse. Lisa didn't understand this impulse. Nor did she show any understanding for my explanation that the man looks equally laughable, lying and panting on top of the woman. For her, intercourse was a serious undertaking, which didn't lose one whit of its seriousness through repetition. I just now realized what a serious situation my life is in. As long as we were living together, Lisa often wanted to prove to me that my modest lifestyle was not of my own choosing. One jacket, one suit, two pairs of pants, four shirts, and two pairs of shoes are the sum of my possessions. To put it bluntly, I have lived and continue to live off of Lisa's pension. To put it equally bluntly, my own income is nothing to speak of. To this day I haven't managed to create a so-called solid financial foundation. I can hardly talk about this problem anymore, although it's getting increasingly urgent with every passing week. Fortunately my parents are no longer living. They'd say flat out that I was averse to work. My father was particularly proud of the fact that he worked from age sixteen up until his death. He had it good. He forgot his conflicts during and because of his work. With me it's exactly the other way around. It's only while and if I am working that I think about my conflicts. For that reason it's better for me to avoid working altogether. People like my parents never had the slightest understanding for this. Lisa was able to understand me, at least for several years. And I took her understanding as unflagging and eternal. But the truth is that it was used up little by little and now it's gone completely. My situation was (is) also difficult because even though she intended it as a pedagogical device, her mocking of my modest means also concealed an affectionate challenge. She had given me permission to withdraw money from her bank account. I used this permission one single time and it was a complete failure. That was about three years ago. I had no trouble withdrawing the money, but afterwards I couldn't bring myself to spend it. When it came time to pay, I was overcome by a dreadful inhibition. I had to return the items I was purchasing and go home. I didn't hide the incident from Lisa. She was moved, and consoled me. She said I took everything far too seriously. That's how understanding she was, back then. Since then I've avoided taking money from her account. We had arranged our daily lives so that either Lisa did the shopping (and therefore would withdraw the necessary money) or, if I were going, she would supply me with enough to buy what we needed, and generally a little extra, so that I could get something for myself as well.

The day is approaching when I shall have to give up my inhibitions concerning Lisa's money, and it won't matter how I go about it. Lisa hasn't closed the account where her pension is deposited. It's just that the deposits for the last two months are missing; obviously there's a new account I don't know about. If I'm interpreting these signs correctly, then Lisa is leaving me the money that has accumulated in the old account, without comment, as a kind of compensation. If I'm thrifty I could live off of it for a good two or even two and a half years. In the meantime I'll finally have to figure out how to stand on my own two feet. At first I was both delighted and hurt by Lisa's generosity. How am I to break up with a woman who takes almost two and a half years to say goodbye, and does so with an almost unimaginable generosity? A while back I realized that the whole thing was also a cleverly engineered scheme. I see how intimidated I am by Lisa's gift. How can you keep your head above water, as a man, if the woman who's giving you money is no longer giving you her good will as well? The shame is so great that right now I don't have the nerve to dial Renate's number and ask for Lisa. Lisa moved out of my life and paid for my silence. She knows I don't have the strength (audacity, stupidity) to break through my shame and put an end to the silence. I would never have believed that Lisa could be so calculating. Naturally I have to wait until this view of events has been corroborated. It's still possible that Lisa will take all the money from the old account and close it out. It could also be that Renate is nudging her in this direction or even pressuring her. After all, Renate told her she ought to ditch me years ago. The telephone is ringing at the other end of the hall. It's probably Habedank, the manager from the Weisshuhn Shoe Factory, who is waiting for my test reports. If I go another few days without calling, I'll be endangering my job. How am I supposed to work up the energy to talk to Habedank right now? When Lisa was still here, the telephone wasn't a problem either. She knew me and she knew my clients; she'd answer the phone and she always understood without asking me what lie to tell which client in order to protect me and my moods. I let the phone ring; I don't know what to say to anyone. At the same time, its ringing is giving me away. Habedank knows my habits; he knows I'm home, he knows I'm spending more time at home, I told him so myself, since I can't control myself the way I used to. The truth is that I find myself craving silence more and more often, and that makes me a little afraid, because I don't know whether the amount of silence I need to live is within normal bounds, or if perhaps it marks the beginning of my inner disease, which is only inadequately described as crumbling apart or unraveling or fraying. I look at the floor and observe the fuzzy bits of dust lying around here and there. How strangely surreptitious, the way the dust multiplies! Suddenly I hit on the perfect description for the present state of my life: fuzzed up. I'm exactly like one of those fuzzy bits of dust—half-transparent, soft on the inside, pliable on the outside, exceedingly clinging and apart from that quiet. I recently came up with the idea of sending a silence schedule to everyone I know—or, to be precise, everyone who knows me. The schedule would list the exact times when I want to speak and when I don't. Anyone who refuses to comply with the silence schedule would no longer be able to speak with me at all. Monday and Tuesday are/would be listed as NON-STOP SILENCE. Wednesdays and Thursdays would have NON-STOP SILENCE only in the morning; the afternoons would be considered RELAXED SILENCE—i.e., short conversations and short phone calls would be permitted. Only on Fridays and Saturdays am I/would I be prepared for unrestrained chitchat, and even then only after eleven o'clock. Sundays would consist of TOTAL SILENCE. Actually I had the silence schedule nearly complete and came within a hair of sending it off. I'd gone so far as to type the addresses on the envelopes. It's a good thing that Lisa will never find out about it. Even hearing the words "silence schedule" would probably be enough to make her cry. Lisa often broke into tears surprisingly easily, but then she'd stop just as quickly. If the phone happened to ring she'd stifle her tears in a matter of seconds and pick up the receiver. If she were here now, she'd say in a steady voice that I was at the dentist's at the moment. Nor would she really be lying, either, since for weeks I've been undergoing a dental treatment that will soon be over, thank God. The new dental assistant called and said in her sunny voice: Your new teeth have arrived! I was instantly rendered speechless. The assistant repeated: Your new teeth are in. I never believed it possible that such a sentence might be addressed to me. The assistant didn't have the slightest awareness that she was a barbarian. And I didn't have the courage to tell her. I stammered some embarrassed half-sentence into the telephone from which the dental assistant could conclude that I would soon come by to pick up my new teeth. But precisely that is highly dubious. It's much more likely that I'll send the dental assistant a silence schedule as well. The sun is flooding the apartment, revealing my fuzzed-up life. During the summer I feel an additional guilt. It stays light until ten in the evening and by five in the morning it's already light again. The days stretch shamelessly along, making it clear to me the extent to which I simply let them slip by. At least the phone has stopped ringing. I'm sure it was Habedank. He's the only one who knows how much every empty ring annoys me. At the same time, it's not all that bad to make an appointment with Habedank. We'd sit in his office for about an hour, chatting with each other, and then he'd give me four or five new assignments. All he needs from me are my test reports, and afterwards he'll want to talk with me about model trains from the fifties and sixties, especially the TRIX and FLEISCHMANN brands. How awful! Model trains! Good God! I never would have believed that those kinds of childish things could possibly become important. But Habedank doesn't have anyone he can talk to about model trains. I ought to call him right away and set up an appointment. But I walk past the phone into the front room. Fate is now unfolding, the unauthorized life. I've always grown melancholy whenever I was supposed to engage in struggle. I'm going to have to struggle, therefore I will grow melancholy. It's as if I were standing up to my knees in some foul stretch of water. Habedank is going to take away my job because I no longer talk with him about model trains. I stand at the window and look down on the street, observing a young man who's cleaning the sidewalk outside the office of a construction firm. He shows up every fourteen days and uses a high-pressure cleaner to blow the leaves that are lying around, first in front of him and then into a specific area. Then he fetches a large blue plastic bag from his car, stuffs the leaves inside, and takes it away. The construction company's mania for tidiness appalls me. I can't believe that the architectural draftsmen and draftswomen, design engineers, and stress analysts attach such importance to having a perfectly cleaned sidewalk! That they can't bear the sight of even a few leaves! I wonder if these ladies and gentlemen were never children who found it fun to kick up a bunch of leaves with the insteps of their shoes, whether the noise they made by doing so and the sight of the piled leaves didn't help them withstand their bewildered mothers or their terrible teachers or the whispers of their poor souls. Or maybe they were never really with it in the first place and that's why they grew up to become such champions of immaculately cleaned sidewalks?

I've just had an idea. I'm going to devise a crash course for Memory Arts. I'll call myself the MNEMOSYNE INSTITUTE, that sounds modern and new and all the nine-to-five fuddy-duddies will want to know what it is. For four or five evenings I'll offer a basic course in the art of remembering. Yes! That's it! I'll talk long and smart until the employees finally grasp how wonderful it was back then, when they used their shoes to make the small piles of leaves bigger and bigger. Then even the most obdurate stress analyst will understand that it's a good thing to walk through rustling leaves and feel that irreplaceable and unparalleled feeling that every human being is always one and the same person with a single chronicle of memory that is slowly but surely growing richer and richer. This insight will do the draftspeople and stress analysts endless good and they'll send the man with the high-pressure cleaner home and invest some of their savings in the newly founded MNEMOSYNE INSTITUTE. And I will earn money with these courses! Good Lord! Money! Suddenly I see the man down on the sidewalk stop, take off one shoe, jiggle his sock back into place, replace the shoe and go back to work. This man puts a stop to my daydream, I don't know why. Probably it's from observing the base certitude that people even feel obliged to keep their shoes in order. I sense that my daydream is leaving me, or more precisely that it is changing, first into a threat and then into an embarrassment. I'm not going to earn any money, at least not with courses on the art of memory. Those last euphoric sentences I spoke into the still-darkened rehearsal room of my future, where they should be able to see for themselves whether they can start anything with my life. Ha! Memory Arts for nine-to-fivers! They won't possibly get it! On the contrary, they'll ask three times how to spell Mnemosyne, because they've never heard the word before. They'll laugh at you! Memory Arts! What's that supposed to mean! My daydream is running away and mocking me as it does so. That's the way they always do, I've known it for a long time. Memory Arts! Only the house mouse across the street could have come up with something like that! To this day fantasies like that still keep me from finally becoming someone who is able to cope with life. I sigh because I am such a small, fallible person. That's the last lesson of the fleeing daydream. Why does your brain keep hatching these rotten eggs that no one wants to buy? Why are you always thinking thoughts that impress only yourself and which you cannot share with anyone (excepting Lisa), because no one (excepting Lisa) understands how a grown man can be convinced that he might be able to earn money with humbug like that. Why do you let a man with a high-pressure cleaner and a few leaves lead you astray like that? When will you finally have an idea that will be illuminating for other people as well? And for which they will pay, and quickly!

# 4

I'M SO EXHAUSTED WITH MYSELF THAT I DECIDE TO GET MY hair cut—at least that way I'll get one sensible thing done today. So I leave my apartment for the second time, since there's no other way for me to escape all these foolish ideas inside my brain. But you can't go on distracting yourself for the rest of your life, I mutter to myself. There must be some other passion for you apart from this eternal craving to disappear. I actually get a little pleasure from listening to my own insults, since their sweet poison also tends to turn them back on themselves; I feel instantly exonerated by the exaggeration lurking inside the invectives. You old baboon, I say to myself, no you looney pants, no pantaloon and once again I have to laugh at the mildness of my self-mockery. In a certain way this early afternoon has made me invulnerable. I still feel the crumbling apart or rather the fuzzing-up inside me, but the whole thing amuses me at the same time, so that I can't really be angry with myself. Margot's hair salon isn't far from my/our apartment. It's one of the many small shops in the district that are practically teetering daily on the edge of the abyss, just like me. In that respect we're very well suited to each other, the small shops and I. At first the only reason I went to Margot's salon was because it made me feel both alienated and amused. Or rather because I didn't see how those two things could go together. I still don't understand the simultaneity of these two effects, but these days I'm even more amused because of my lack of understanding, at least when it's about as trivial or perhaps even preposterous a place as a hair salon. Margot's was outfitted in the 1960s and presumably hasn't been remodeled since. The men's section has three clunky, overly ornate porcelain shampoo bowls that easily overpower the little room. Apart from Margot there are no other hairdressers or barbers. And presumably Margot doesn't have more than a few clients—a handful of older ladies and people like myself who don't want to pay too much. The first time I walked in, Margot was sitting with her head bent over the empty middle sink. Only when I came closer did I see that she was eating a bowl of soup, which she had placed deep inside the basin. Margot was a little frightened and taken aback. Evidently she hadn't counted on any more customers and had forgotten to lock the door. I offered to leave, but Margot asked me to stay and took away the half-eaten bowl of soup. Today she isn't eating soup. Instead, there's a cat sleeping in the same middle sink.

You're in luck, says Margot, I can take care of you right away. The cat refuses to be bothered by the sudden commotion. Margot walks over to the barber chair on the far left and spins it so the seat is facing me; I sit down. There are a few drawings on the wall between the mirrors—evidently done by Margot herself. They all show the same profile of a woman, with her hair in a kind of bob. For a moment the drawings remind me of my mother, who in her last years enjoyed painting a similar head with a bobbed hairdo. Margot covers my front with a fresh apron. I'm the only customer. Margot says: By now I can recognize you by the back of your head. We have a quick laugh, then Margot hands me a magazine with the title *Lucky Break*. The partition separating the men's section from the women's looks even older than the other furnishings. It's a crisscross lattice made of bamboo, the kind you could see in many apartments during the 1960s. Three flowerpots resting in terra-cotta bowls hang from the partition, attached to the latticework with raffia bows. Margot switches on the portable radio. Pop music fills the room; the cat glances up. In *Lucky Break* I read the beginning of a feature on the progeny of the Swedish royal house. The headline states: THE ROYAL HEIR

IS HERE. I misread it as THE ROYAL HAIR IS HERE. But even though this hair salon is far from royal—quite the contrary—I'm fascinated by its jumbled hodgepodge. Margot reminds me of the women I knew before Lisa. None of them really suited me. Back then I gave up on the idea that a "right" woman actually existed somewhere, and steeled myself against the suffering that comes from being with an unsuitable woman. Shortly after that I met Lisa. Now Lisa's gone and I wonder whether I won't again have to steel myself against women who don't suit me, women I'm only with because there aren't any others. At the same time I'm not looking to start up some new romance, either with a suitable woman or with an unsuitable one, but then, I'm not entirely sure of this. Margot wets my hair as she tells me about her ill-fated vacation on the Baltic. Hardly a day went by without her mother complaining about the bad weather, the bad service, and the bad mood of the staff. In the end, says Margot, I wound up complaining about the weather, the service, and the staff myself, though in reality I couldn't care less about things like that. That's the last time I'm going on vacation with my mother. We laugh. Margot carefully removes my glasses and trims the hair that's grown out over my ears. Now she's talking about her brother being an embezzler, which I already heard about on an earlier visit. Fifteen minutes later she's waving a circular hand mirror behind my head. I nod and say to my freshly cut hair: That's great, terrific. My exaggerated commentary is a clear sign that I won't be going home right away. Margot whisks the hair off my neck and shoves the clippings off the apron onto the floor. She unties the apron and shaves the back of my neck. The cat cranes its head; Margot turns off the portable radio. At the cash register we kiss, just like we did last time, some three weeks ago. I'm still not looking for any new romance. I don't believe I'm capable of saying or hearing all the sentences that have to be spoken in the course of an

affair. But Margot makes it easy for me. Not that she does-
n't talk a lot, relatively speaking, but it's not the usual love
babble. I put away my wallet. Margot locks the door to the
shop; I follow her back to the room adjoining the women's
section. It's not the first time we've slept together right after
a haircut. The blinds are halfway down behind the drawn
net curtains. I look out onto an empty courtyard. Last time
a few children were playing there, but today all I see is a
small birdcage in the window of a building off to the side.
Only now do I realize that my glasses are probably still on
the edge of the sink. Without my glasses I can't tell that the
two birds in the cage are birds; all I can see are two moving
spots. Because I don't have my glasses, the situation strikes
me as both intimate and strange. It's only at home that I
allow myself to take off my glasses for any length of time.
Wandering about and looking around without my glasses
serves for me as a kind of authorization for my life that's
crumbling apart. Margot has already undressed. It doesn't
occur to me that she might be in a hurry. She helps me
unbutton my shirt and unlace my shoes. If I'm not mistak-
en, it doesn't really matter to Margot that I might not be in
the mood. She reminds me of the kind of men people are
always saying sleep with their wives even when the latter
don't really want to. I think I sense that she enjoys helping
me undress. It's clear that she appreciates breaking up her
long workday with the odd affair. Just like last time, she sits
down on the couch, pulls me towards her and starts sucking
my cock. I glance back and forth between the two moving
spots in the window across the courtyard and the three dry-
ers in the women's section. The plexiglas domes are chipped
and discolored. I look down at the petite woman on the
couch; at the moment I find Margot very attractive.
Although I don't need any support, I keep a firm grip on her
shoulders. Twice I bend over slightly and reach for her firm
little breasts. All of a sudden I think about my course for

Memory Arts. At about the same time I realize that the whole idea is really nothing more than an expression of my personal wish for my own private sea of leaves, which I may traipse through all alone. Presumably being together with Margot has helped me discern my ulterior motive behind the memory course. In any case I never would have gotten to the heart of the matter without her. A current of gratitude passes through me and I stroke her back, as though I'd just discovered that Margot gets cold before and during intercourse exactly like Lisa. My gratitude also shows itself in my penis, which has become unusually large and rigid. And suddenly it dawns on me that all I have to do is fill Lisa's empty room with leaves, and I'll have my own private leaf reserve. Wouldn't that be an excellent technique for separating from Lisa, and for simultaneously understanding that I can never really separate from her completely? All I have to do is fill a few plastic bags with sycamore leaves, sneak them into the apartment, and spread them in Lisa's room, that's it. I play with this idea for a few seconds and feel happy. I don't know whether this happiness is a new lucky break thanks to Margot, or whether it's still the old happiness left over from Lisa. At the same time, I'm worried that I'll wind up *non compos mentis*, sitting in Lisa's room surrounded by countless wilted leaves, jabbering away in a state of confusion, the same words over and over—that I'm no longer prepared to put up with an unauthorized life. As usual, no one will understand. Except for Lisa, of course, but Lisa isn't there and never will be there again. She won't visit me until I'm locked up in an institution, but even then she won't understand me because she's bound to cry and lose all her strength. A psychiatrist will talk about disintegrative ego disorders, depressive agitation with psychotic symptoms, a paranoid persecution complex. The newspapers are always full of words like that whenever there's an incident involving someone who doesn't know what's what and has to be taken in. Lisa will listen to words like that and will cry even harder. Margot lets go of me and gets up on her knees, bending forward on the couch. I grope for her sex with my hands and feel that she's dry. I moisten my index finger and middle finger with spit and tenderly rub her labia. Then I do the same thing with my ring finger and little finger. Carefully and slowly I shove my smokestack into Margot's pudenda. With both hands I grab her small, child-sized ass and pull her firmly towards me. Margot lets out a few animal grunts, which I enjoy hearing. Fortunately I manage to prolong the intercourse by keeping my movements as uniform as possible. For the first time I wonder briefly whether I couldn't see Margot outside the hair salon. Suddenly I'm worried that I might soon be ashamed of having once been healthy. And soon after that I actually lose a bit of that health; a few seconds later it becomes clear that I won't be having an orgasm. Evidently it's the same with Margot. Restlessly she props herself up, first on her hands, then back on her elbows. She's still bent over forward, but unexpectedly turns back and looks at me. I take her glance as permission to break off. I free myself from Margot, she gets up and for a couple of moments projects a beautiful sense of helplessness. The truncated coitus has made Margot closer to me than she was before. She makes no fuss at all concerning our mishap. I can't tell her how thankful I am. How strange, this being human! If we could be normal, then the strange would be normal, but only rarely can we be normal. I'd like to tell Margot this, but unfortunately I feel guilty and don't say a thing. Thanks to Margot, our interrupted intercourse has resulted in a kind of economy of sadness. This frees up a certain measure of joy which Margot and I share as we look at each other. It's as if we'd already negotiated and kept a number of difficult agreements. Margot is dressed before I am. In my half-clad state I don't dare venture out into the salon to search for my glasses. Margot arranges the room the way it looked before. Until today I'd never given her any money. But now I have the yen to leave a little something here. It shouldn't look as if I wanted to pay her. It's just that Margot's life suddenly makes me feel sorry. She, too, is living an unlicensed life—I can feel it. I sense a need to talk with her about unauthorized living. I can see in her hasty movements the embarrassment that comes from too often feeling merely compelled to live. Still, I'm afraid that at the moment I'm not really up to a conversation about unauthorized life. It would probably make me feel the way I did as a child, hardly ever understanding more than the beginning of whatever was going on. And after I understood the beginning I'd probably escape, remembering all too well how frightened I always was of life's complexities. I see that Margot wants to reopen the salon. The cat wanders into the back room and watches me tie my shoes. Now she jumps onto the couch where Margot was kneeling. My glasses are still perched on the edge of the middle sink. In the neighboring bowl I discover a single dark hair snaking across the porcelain to the edge. In one movement I put on my glasses and take out my wallet. I place a hundred fifty marks down on the counter and signal to Margot that I'm not expecting any change. She doesn't resist. A little while later she opens the door. I brush my lips across Margot's face and disappear.

Out on the street I'm struck by the sight of a man whose shirt collar is too big for him. I'd like to ask him if he's lost all desire to buy shirts that fit. Then I could tell him that I, too, have suffered a similar loss. After that we could go to a pub and—no, that wouldn't happen. On the fourth floor of a building opposite, a young man is playing his accordion next to an open window, for the benefit of the street below. I look up at him, and he responds by playing with renewed enthusiasm, which is slightly embarrassing to me. An infant sleeping in a stroller is pushed past me, every bit as motionless as a little dead man. Swallows in groups of six fly over a nearly deserted intersection. I take in all these details with an exaggerated attentiveness, because I have to work hard not to bend over and start picking up leaves off the ground. For my home, my private leaf reserve. And I realize that the leaf reserve is an idea I'll be able to plan but never carry out. I can only love the leaves as long as they're on the street. I can never allow myself to think that I could save the leaves or myself by spreading some of them around in Lisa's former room. But I also don't want any part of the shame involved in such fruitless wishing. The fear of going insane is so strong at this moment that I'm worried it alone might be enough to trigger madness. Then I bend over and in one swoop grab four, no five hefty sycamore leaves with finely serrated edges and long stems.

# 5

THERE'S NOT A SOUL ON THE EMBANKMENT APART FROM me. A heavily trafficked expressway stretches off to my right. I can hear the persistent drone of the cars, but that hardly bothers me. On my left the river burbles along, a bit silty today, almost muddy; it must have rained in the night. The river is separated from the road by a broad swath of grass, which is crisscrossed by several dirt paths packed hard by frequent use. A few benches are still standing alongside the slightly elevated expressway. Most have been torn out and smashed up by hoodlums in recent years. The city administration chooses not to replace them, which doesn't do much for the looks of the neighborhood. But the neglect along the embankment suits me fine, since I can go about my business here unobserved. I've been working as a shoe tester for seven years, and I can say that it's the only occupation I've ever had that I've been able to pursue with any loyalty. I've even experienced a growing success, which is due not so much to any special talent or ability on my part as to what Habedank, my immediate supervisor, likes to call "our product's favorable market destiny." I work for a small but rapidly expanding manufacturer of luxury shoes, which I found out about through Ipach, a friend of mine at the time. Ipach really wanted to become a stage director, and nearly succeeded, but after too long a stint as directorial assistant at the Oldenburg Municipal Theater he couldn't find a new engagement. By chance he became a salesman for the same shoe manufacturer that is my present employer. All you have to do is spend the whole day walking around in brand new shoes and then write as detailed a report as possible about your sensations while walking. As soon as Ipach told me that, I hopped onto the streetcar and went looking for Habedank, the manager, armed with Ipach's recommendation. Today I'm testing a heavy, hand-sewn welted oxford constructed of polished vegetable-tanned boxcalf leather. Its classic, closed-lacing stays are symmetrical down to the last millimeter. Because of the thickness of the soles, oxfords often feel a little hard (despite the calf leather). I've been walking around in these oxfords for a good hour, but this time I don't detect any uncomfortable pressure spots forming. Presumably this is thanks to the molded cork inserts and the almost tender way they were set by Zappke, the cutter. The second shoes I'm testing today are wingtip brogues—as heavy as the oxfords and similarly welted—not my personal favorite, but a shoe that's regaining popularity among many men. The punching is conventional, at least on the vamp. For the counter, however, the cutter thought up a new pattern, which will presumably add fifty marks to the price of the shoe. The punching is the same color (Bordeaux red) as the upper leather, which may meet with disapproval from some purists. Of course these same purists will also object to the Bordeaux red, because in their opinion a shoe that expensive and that respectable must be either black or brown (dark brown). The third pair are some cordovan (horse leather) bluchers, the most expensive shoes available today. The uppers are constructed from an extremely high number of individually hand-sewn pieces. The edges of some of these pieces are exposed, while others are hidden inside the shoe. The blucher is as soft as a woolen cap and despite the number of discrete pieces, it wears like a unified whole. Among the three pairs of shoes I'll give it the best evaluation. Habedank insists that I test each pair for at least four days. But it's been years since I've done that. By now it doesn't take me more than half a day to get a clear picture of a shoe's walking quality and write up an accurate report, with a particular focus on the places where the heel or toes might feel pinched. I sit down in the grass and look at the river, which is at once bleak and calming, as it presses ahead, slow and wide, glittering and shimmering in the sunlight like an open chest of silverware.

Not far from here a narrow footbridge bends over the river. A pair of lovers is walking across. When they're almost at the middle they stop and kiss—a trace too energetically. It's as if they'd suddenly felt threatened and kissed in order to ward off the threat. Now the couple has finished kissing; they look relieved, and step off the narrow bridge in high spirits. An exceedingly unkempt woman appears from the left, coming along the dirt path. She's between fifty and sixty years old, with a suitcase in her left hand. Her clothes, shoes, and hair are dirty and partially matted, respectively. I try hard not to pay attention to her, though that doesn't exactly reflect my inner truth. The fact is, I enjoy being around people who are confused, half-crazy, or completely nuts, and imagining that I'll soon be one of them. Then I'd be exempted from finally having to find stable employment and from having to mold my life to fit this stable employment. And as soon as I'm confused myself, I will at last have the strength to finish off and do away with whatever doesn't fit into this life that was so long in the finding. The woman walks up and lays her suitcase down in the grass in front of me—an old cardboard trunk with a tin-plated handle. It occurs to me that the last thing left of a person is their suitcase, which, if it isn't wantonly destroyed, will last forever. And suitcase handles are even more indestructible than the suitcases themselves. Long after this woman is dead and her suitcase destroyed, the metal handle will remain as a reminder of a life rendered unrecognizable. I'd like to tell the woman: Rest assured, your suitcase handle will always bear witness to your life. I can't bring myself to say those words. For that reason, it would be (is) now appropriate for my eyes to start tearing up. But my face stays dry. The woman opens her suitcase and shows me its emptiness. All I can see are two loose straps that just hang there while the woman fiddles with them. I'm sure that the empty suitcase is the reason for the kissing couple's sudden fear. They must have seen the woman with the suitcase while they were still on the bridge, and had the unambiguous perception that they themselves would soon be nothing more than two halves of an empty suitcase. The woman giggles, snaps her suitcase shut, and walks off. A few seconds later I think about my mother. When I was a child, she would often arrange her handbag, hat, scarf and umbrella on the dresser a little before noon, as if she were about to go out. But then she wouldn't go out. She'd sit down in the chair beside the telephone and look at her handbag, hat, scarf and umbrella. After a while I would join her, and together we would look at the things that had been arranged for going out but not used. Half a minute later my mother and I would hug, pressing each other tightly, laughing right in each other's faces. Today I assume that this was how my mother controlled her own shock at the fact that the world didn't seem worth seeing. My reminiscing gives rise to a sense of humble contentment. For a moment I think I'll be perfectly satisfied if I can sit here and watch the river once or twice a week. A brimstone butterfly flutters over the tips of the grass. I never was very interested in whether there was such a thing as a soul or not, but all of a sudden I find myself playing with the thought that I might have one. In truth, however, I don't know what a soul is, or how you could talk about souls without embarrassment. But I'd like to know what I have to do to keep it safe from harm. Keep it safe from harm! Yes, that's exactly what's going through my head and I'm not ashamed by the pathetic simple-mindedness of the thought. Soul is probably another word for imperviousness—a small colorful merry-go-round I'm always on the verge of jumping aboard whenever I sit here in the grass. The soul doesn't say anything to that, but I notice how it's always on the verge of saying something. Most likely it won't ever say anything, it will only show a few images: the anxious couple kissing, the empty suitcase, the memory of my mother. At the moment I'm solely focused on the fluff that keeps forming in my jacket pocket. I didn't go crazy during the night. I took the sycamore leaves I had collected on the street and spread them in Lisa's room. I looked at the leaves for a long time, and I was pleased. I wonder whether it's good to pick leaves from one specific tree or if I should take leaves from several different trees into my apartment. Right now I'm feeling a little daunted by that prospect because it's almost noon and I'm hungry. I have to save money and would like to forgo frequenting expensive restaurants. Of course I've also had enough of bistros and stand-up snack bars. I'm still shaking after what happened to me a few days ago.

Around 1 p.m. I walked into a fast food cafeteria and took my place in a line of hungry people. I quickly noticed that the woman behind the counter wasn't looking at the people she was serving. She didn't even bother to look up, just kept saying *Next* every time she set a plate on the glass counter. The unlooked-at people hastily took their allotted portions and spread out among the little stand-up tables. At that point I realized that the woman's refusal to look at the diners meant that they also refused to look at one another. But it wasn't until I was setting my plate down that the scary truth really hit me: here I was once again in a cheap cafeteria getting the cheap daily special. Ashamed, I rushed to finish my meal. I was so embarrassed that I closed my eyes each time I shoved the fork into my mouth. But closing and reopening my eyes like that made me seem affected. And a few minutes later the affectation forced me to stop eating. I acted as if the daily special wasn't good enough for me. Like a bad actor, I shoved the plate to the middle of the little table and spun around. As I did so I noticed that at least two

of the diners weren't taking my pompous behavior seriously. They had secretly noticed that I—oh I don't know what
they'd noticed. In any case, I can't let that kind of thing happen to me again. Even when you live elbow-to-elbow with
other people, you need to have the imperturbable conviction of a monk. I give a little moan as I stand and brush a
few blades of grass off my jacket. I've decided to test the
horse-leather shoes on my way home. After just a few steps
I notice that there's hardly anything I lack more than the
imperturbable conviction of a monk. My humble contentment has changed its name after a long period of looking
around and about. Now it's called procrastination, and it
may give me an entirely new fright under this name. It's
true, I'm too lethargic. My fussiness and my distractibility
will be the death of me. Meanwhile, there's no one I can
complain to about these traits. I have no choice but to
accept them and hope that over time they lose a little of
their intractability. But time passes, and the traits remain.
With almost every passing week they grow increasingly
impossible. I have to put an end to my absentmindedness
and yet I realize that I can't live without it. It's clear that this
conflict will either squeeze the breath out of me or else
make me sick, which in my case is one and the same thing.
What's more, I can't figure out why *my* life in particular has
to be the site of such a base conflict. For decades I've tried
very hard to live without quarrels, and for a long time I was
successful. I made my earliest attempts at constructing a
harmonious daily routine when I was still a child. The first
years of my life passed according to this model: I got up in
the morning, played in my pajamas for a while and then ate
breakfast with my mother. After that I'd go outside for half
an hour, meet my friends at the playground and wander
around the nearby riverbank—which I'm just now leaving—
with one or two of them. Then I'd split off from my friends,
go home, and enjoy a friendly reception from my mother.

The next day it was the same thing all over again. And that's more or less how my life went in the early years. My mother seemed to be in agreement with this arrangement, but that wasn't the case. Because she was the one who put an end to my peaceful life with her at home by sticking me in a kindergarten. All of a sudden I was surrounded by twenty-six children I didn't know and never wanted to get to know. For the first time there was something I didn't understand. That is to say, I couldn't make it jibe with everything I thought I had understood about life until then. So I broke off that attempt at understanding and looked for another beginning that would better fit what I had already understood. That's how I came to think that I hardly ever understand any more than the beginning of whatever is going on. Before long I was tangled up in layer after layer of nascent understandings—though of what I could no longer say. To this day, whenever things get too complicated and I'm forced to make another start at understanding something, I break off the attempt, or rather I fall into a mood of child-like waiting. The problem is, my mind gets cluttered with vast amounts of partially understood material. I walk through the straw grass of the embankment, which the sun's rays have parched so that they're practically brittle. As a child I would roam through the area by myself or with two friends and all I felt was the grass brushing against my knees. I took care not to run into any nettles, I loved the word rhubarb, and I began feeding on sorrel and dandelion. As soon as I started wandering around here, I sank into an inner reverie I couldn't find anywhere else. Because the grass all around me was something I didn't have to understand. Presumably in those hours I wandered inconceivably far into the peculiarities of my life that continue to this day. Whatever lasts must ultimately grow strange. I leave the embankment behind me and turn left towards the highway. I'll buy a small loaf of bread and a package of spaghetti in a supermarket. I've taken to buying only two foodstuffs at a time—for instance, fruit and butter, milk and coffee, or bread and spaghetti. These days any purchase that costs more than ten marks is cause for alarm. If, on the other hand, I only take two foodstuffs home, I have the feeling of having behaved well once again. A new household goods store is opening on Dürer Strasse. Balloons dangle above the entrance, an employee dressed as a circus ringmaster plays a barrel organ, one lady offers canapés to the passersby, while another serves champagne. I can feel the allure of public drunkenness; I'm already holding my second glass. The canapés are garnished with cold roast pork, ham, and smoked salmon. If I play my cards right, I could solve the problem of my midday meal here in a trice, and at the store's expense. Besides, I've taken an interest in a young man with Down's syndrome, who claps his hands as he twirls to the music from the barrel organ. Like many disabled people, he's wearing striped socks and a sweater that's much too small for him. The employees of the household goods store aren't blind to the fact that people are more interested in the disabled man than in the opening. I like his happy/vacant face, his guileless expression, his bear-like satisfaction. Everyone else is struggling with something; only the disabled man is basking in the happiness of his difference. I take a second slice of white bread with some roast pork. The disabled man wants some of the champagne but an older woman, probably his mother, abruptly takes his glass away. He seems not to notice the reproach and goes on dancing. A saleslady asks if I'd like to see the gift department. I'd be happy to, I say, annoyed that I'm allowing myself to be so quickly distracted from my interests. But then Susanne steps up from behind and saves me.

Either we never see each other at all or else we see each other all the time, she declares, squeezing in between the saleslady and myself.

And neither seems like a very good option, does it? I say, offering Susanne my glass.

What are you doing here anyway? Susanne asks.

I'm wondering whether I should turn this PR event into a full-fledged meal.

Almost everybody here is thinking the same thing, says Susanne.

You too?

No, says Susanne, I'm going to NUDELHOLZ, don't you want to come along?

Is that a restaurant?

Yes, very nice and not expensive.

I give my champagne glass back to the saleslady and set off with Susanne.

They keep a table free for me, says Susanne, since I eat there two or three times a week.

I manage to stow my test shoes a little deeper in my canvas bag, since I don't want to talk about my job, at least not now. Susanne is wearing a close-fitting dark blouse and a stylish gray skirt with a few black buttons on the side pleat. Her bosom has grown more ample in recent years. Little gaps have formed between her incisors. She walks ahead of me with a snappy gait and complains about her colleagues.

You wouldn't believe what a lot of boring dolts lawyers can be.

I watch a young couple kneeling next to a stroller as they share a bratwurst with their child. Susanne moves the tip of her tongue from the left corner of her mouth to the right corner and back again. Even when she isn't speaking she doesn't close her lips. The indignation behind her words lends form and urgency to her face. NUDELHOLZ is small to the point of being cramped. Some two dozen tables are set up in a single elongated room—approximately half are occupied. We take a seat close to the window; I read the menu. Susanne is still railing against the lawyers at work. At the next table an elderly man has dropped a potato onto the floor; I watch as he tries to shove it under his table with the tip of his right shoe. I wonder whether Susanne will change the subject if I call her attention to the man. Instead, she says to me: If you've decided what you're having you should close the menu so the waiter knows he can come to our table. Obediently, I close the menu. My gaze rests fixedly on the fallen potato. A little while later Susanne apologizes.

Don't hold what I said against me, she says, I just had a few too many insights into the baseness of life this morning.

That's ok, I reply.

Susanne takes a few swallows of water and watches the people passing outside.

The misery of the masses, says Susanne (she really says that: The misery of the masses. I'm amazed) lies in the fact that all these poor people have never met an important person in their life. You understand?

I nod and drink some water myself.

All these Wenzels and Schrothoffs and Seidels (those are the names of her colleagues) know are other Wenzels, Schrothoffs and Seidels, and that's what makes them all such champions of the ordinary.

I agree with her wholeheartedly.

Susanne orders pasta mista; I content myself with a reasonably priced risotto.

I feel threatened by all this mediocrity as well, says Susanne, though I go out of my way to avoid anything that's ordinary. Sometimes I sit in bed in the evening and have to cry because I can't ever act again. It's the same with my friend Christa. The things that she planned to do! She wanted to study philosophy, go on long trips. Now she's sitting on the shore of some stinking quarry pond reading the TV guide! Not to mention Martina! She spends her money on clothes and cosmetics while she's running after a younger man who doesn't even want her cleaning his

51

kitchen! And what about Himmelsbach! You know him too, right?

I nod.

Himmelsbach is a disaster! Susanne exclaims. And to think I even admired him! Going off to Paris so he could take photos for international magazines! What a joke!

I saw him recently, I say. I think he's in a bad way.

It's terrible, says Susanne, now I don't know anyone important either.

I expect Susanne to blurt out right in my face: And that includes you! Instead, she tells me about two women with advanced degrees in German who recently started working in her office as secretaries.

They talk as if they'd always been secretaries, says Susanne.

I'd like to pay Susanne a compliment, but I'm afraid that right now it would sound like a consolation. Susanne sighs and looks down at her matte pearl necklace.

It's a good thing I have to work this afternoon, otherwise I'd get drunk.

Why's that? I ask, quietly.

Because I'm so depressed.

And how, I ask, would you insure that the masses have regular contact with important people?

Susanne looks at me.

Do you want to equip every apartment house with one important man or woman, and give them office hours from ten to one every day except Thursday? Or should some important man make a weekly appearance in the town hall to talk about importance and how to acquire it?

Susanne laughs out loud. You're not taking me seriously!

Of course I'm taking you seriously! I'm just wondering how the masses might have contact with important people. After all, you said yourself there's not enough of that.

But I didn't mean it that way, says Susanne.

Then how did you mean it?

OK, says Susanne, somewhat disdainfully, I see I've just been dreaming out loud again. But thank God that with you I can at least talk about all my nonsense!

Susanne laughs. We raise our glasses and drink. I'm glad that she changed the mood, which was getting a little too serious. Although in actuality, as far as Susanne is concerned, my personal situation may be more serious than before. Her remark that at least with me she can talk about her dreaming nonsense, or her nonsensical dreams, now strikes me as a sign that she doesn't find me average after all. We settle up and leave. I accompany her back to her office.

Did you hear what I said? Susanne asks outside. You're the only person I can share my bizarre complaints with!

She pauses and looks at me a tad too dramatically. I nod. If I start getting involved with Susanne I'll probably experience this kind of scene more and more frequently. I'm already thinking about the fact that I still don't feel any special desire for a woman. Actually that's a bit of an oversimplification. Of course I want a woman, but at forty-six I feel that I'm too old or too used up to play the lover one more time. I can't talk like that kind of man anymore; I can't act like that kind of man anymore. It's just a coincidence that I've gotten closer to Susanne again. But even this coincidental closeness is enough for me to sense who Susanne is really waiting for: a competent, successful, interesting man. The man who happens to be present (me) spends time with her and observes that the man of her desires/longings/dreams is not appearing in her life. That's the only reason that the Susanne who's left where she is spends her time with the man who happens to be there—in other words, me. All this is aggravated by the fact that Susanne is essentially too beautiful for me. Truly beautiful women always lead me to a single thought: You're not good enough for her. It's only with women who aren't so pretty or intelligent that I think: They're like me, they won't be shocked if I pay attention to them. Even so, I'm walking like a man who wants to make sure Susanne doesn't have to step aside to avoid oncoming pedestrians. Susanne is telling me that she has to prepare the files this afternoon for a trial her firm is handling tomorrow morning at the provincial courthouse. Her voice has a tinge of disparagement. Now we're walking into the sun. Susanne takes a pair of black sunglasses out of her bag and puts them on. Her lamentations win me over strongly to her side. Just now she really does look like an actress who doesn't want anyone to ever again allude to her earlier successes. I should forget that Susanne really had just *one* engagement, and even that wasn't a genuine engagement. She was twenty-four years old and had a lover who was equally young and essentially without a profession but considered himself to be a future man of the theater. He used his inheritance (his father was a dentist) to start a small studio theater and let Susanne perform there. He was as much a layman as she was—two amateurs appearing on stage as professionals, unchecked by reality. For a while, that is—after about two years reality began to intrude. The lover's fortune was spent, the patrons had not materialized, the theater had to shut down. And that was the end of Susanne's playacting. But at the moment it looks as though the whole story never happened. Susanne struts ahead with quick steps and a smoldering melancholy. It's as if her grief might at any time force her to relive her story all over again. But now, says Susanne in front of the doors of her firm, it's back to reality! She laughs quickly, turns around, and is gone.

I head on towards the market near Rhein Strasse, where there are a few stands with livestock. I plan to sit on a bench and mull over what I should do. Susanne probably doesn't know herself whether she ought to consider me ordinary or maybe even important. Just before I reach Rhein Strasse I see

Scheuermann, my former piano teacher, walking my way. He slows down, perhaps he wants to speak with me, but I manage to avoid him. About twenty-two years ago Scheuermann gave me a single piano lesson. It could have been more, but after the first hour I was so embarrassed by myself that I declared an end to my piano instruction. Presumably to this day Scheuermann wants to tell me I shouldn't have been so hard on myself and that I can resume my instruction at any time. Rhein Strasse exudes an odor of hairspray, gasoline, bratwurst, smoke and chicken excrement. Above the noise of the traffic I can hear the peeping of the chicks confined to flat cages on the ground. I sit down on a bench near one of the stands with geese and chickens. There's not a soul in sight to shoo away my distressing thoughts about whether or not I'm important enough for Susanne. But really, the answer is very simple: in terms of education I am, but in terms of occupation I'm not. The only truly important people are the ones who have been able to fuse their individual knowledge with their position in life. Outsiders like me, who are merely educated, are nothing more than modern-day beggars who have never been told their place. In order to recover from this foolish conversation with myself, I watch an older handicapped woman parking her wheelchair underneath an awning. She eats a bratwurst sitting down. I'm confused to find myself wondering after so many years whether or not I should get closer to Susanne. And to think that what sparked this wondering was nothing more than a chance meeting during Susanne's lunch break. I know her bosom, so to speak, from childhood, but haven't seen it or touched it for many years, so perhaps I can no longer claim I really know it. What a strange idea, anyway—wanting to "know" a woman's bosom! In the midst of all this I lose the courage to find life worth continuing. Perhaps I ought to eat a bratwurst myself. I'm not hungry anymore, but perhaps demolishing a bratwurst would help me find the right word for the collective peculiarity of all life. I'm not the only person who watches small animals when his own life is at a standstill. Looking at some of these men and women, it's easy to tell from their strained expressions that they have no intention of ever buying a chicken. They are simply biding their time mutely in front of the cages, hoping for a sudden flash of insight. For half a minute now two older women have been sitting next to me on the bench discussing balcony flowers and problems with fertilizer.

Only ivy is winter hardy.

I know, says the other, but ivy grows too fast for me.

I don't want to listen to the women's conversation and so I wander around a little. At one of the poultry stands, a woman farmer presses one or two tomatoes against the wires of each cage, and the animals inside the cages quickly peck them apart. Suddenly the words winter hardy come back into my consciousness. I ask myself if *I* am winter hardy. No, I'm not—on the contrary, I was always a long way from winter hardiness, I'm not even summer hardy! Of course *with* a woman I am/would be slightly more winter hardy than without. Is it possible that these two words I just happened to hear, winter hardy, will tip the scales for me so that I can again turn my attentions to Susanne? Once more the collective peculiarity of all life courses through me. It's starting to drizzle. I move under the awning where the handicapped woman is still parked. By now she's finished her bratwurst. Without moving, she watches the constantly twitching comb of a rooster. Then she opens her purse and pulls out a sheet of plastic. She unfolds it and wraps it all around her. It doesn't bother her that it's only a few drops she is protecting herself against so vehemently. Finally she pulls a plastic hood over her head and switches on her wheelchair's electric motor. And away she whirrs, an enormously lumpy picture. I follow her with my eyes as long as I can. Then I go home. I have to finish typing the report for Habedank as soon as possible, and I have the feeling I'll manage it this afternoon. I'm even looking forward to getting home, which hasn't been the case for a long time. But when my reason for being tired is halfway respectable, as it is now, I can stop viewing my life with such suspicion.

# 6

SHORTLY AFTER BREAKFAST I LEAVE MY APARTMENT, CARRYING two canvas bags. Each bag contains three pairs of shoes that I have personally tested; the bag in my left hand also holds six evaluation reports, each between two and two-and-a-half pages long. The summer morning is warm and almost excessively bright. The swallows fly straight up the walls of the apartment houses and then either turn sideways over the roofs or soar on into the blue. I'd like to stay right there and at least watch them, if I can't imitate them. But I have an appointment. I'm supposed to meet Habedank at ten. At Ebert Platz I take the number 7 train to Hollenstein, where the Weisshuhn Shoe Factory is located, not far from the station. I'll meet Habedank in the manager's office and give him the shoes along with the reports. We'll chat for about three quarters of an hour—first twenty minutes about the test shoes, and the rest of the time about electric trains. Then Habedank will hand me three or four pairs of new shoes, and I'll go home. I've known this routine for years, but I still get a little nervous every time. It goes back to my particular conceit, which I sense a little more acutely during these expeditions than usual, when I'm just at home. I inherited this conceit from my mother. We both believe that it's not worth looking at the world for an entire lifetime. I used to struggle against the effects of this conceit, but not anymore. Naturally I have to make a special effort when I'm with Habedank. He shouldn't notice my conceit at all. He thinks that I'm an electric train hobbyist just like he is, that to this day I read the same technical magazines that he does, primarily about early TRIX and FLEISCHMANN products. He doesn't realize that I'm just drawing on the same store of

knowledge frozen from my childhood days, and all just for him, time after time. It's also possible that Habedank will tell me one of his tedious stories, which I listen to with perfunctory sympathy. Three weeks ago he took nearly ten minutes to tell me about the end of his vacation. On the whole trip from Italy to Germany he thought he was about to run out of gas. But then he made it back home without incident. That was/is his entire story. I sat still in front of his desk for ten minutes and laughed with delight when he reached the end and exclaimed: It turned out there was enough gas! Imagine! There was enough gas! My conceit entails a nearly continuous collision of humility and disgust. The two forces are of nearly equal strength. On one hand, I sense my humility admonishing: It's precisely the most idiotic stories of your fellow man that you should listen to! At the same time, however, my disgust taunts me: If you don't escape right away, you'll drown in the vapors of your fellow man. What's infuriating is that this constant colliding never allows either side to win. So the two forces just go on running the same collision course over and over. And those are my feelings as I find myself approaching Habedank's office. I tell myself that I'm prepared for anything and right away I have to laugh at myself. Habedank and Oppau, one of the firm's buyers, succeeded in making the office a no-smoking zone. That's why Frau Fischedick, another buyer who still smokes, paces up and down outside the office, smoking and grinning. She holds up her arms and waves at me. I observe that Frau Fischedick wants to be in the office when I speak with Habedank. She puts out her cigarette and goes in shortly after I do.

Habedank is sitting at his long black desk; when he sees me he stands up.

Ah there he is! Our master tester! he calls out.

My conceit triggers a hint of a smile. I walk across a soft gray carpet. The walls are lined with a series of indirect lighting fixtures. The window blinds are closed; the room is cast in gently dimmed light. Herr Oppau's desk is on the left; Frau Fischedick's is on the right, in front of Habedank's. When he opens his jacket I catch sight of a hand-sized bloodstain on the chest of his shirt. I stare at Habedank; Habedank stares at me.

Unfortunately someone took a shot at me, says Habedank.

Who? I ask.

A fired tester.

Oh, I say.

Herr Habedank, Herr Habedank, says Frau Fischedick.

How do you like the bloodbath? asks Habedank and sinks back into his swivel armchair.

Don't believe a word he says! says Frau Fischedick.

Herr Habedank is one of the many people who have earned a natural death, says Herr Oppau.

Savoring that last remark, I sit down in the visitor's chair and place my evaluations on Habedank's table.

A felt-tip pen happened to leak in my shirt pocket, says Habedank.

I don't know what to say to that. Habedank leafs through the evaluations. I reach into my bags and take out a pair of hand-stitched wingtip brogues as well as the cordovans, and explain at length why I consider them to be the best of the latest batch. Habedank, Oppau and Frau Fischedick listen to my report. I let myself believe that it's a pleasure hearing me talk about shoes. Presumably it's no accident that I talk about shoes as if they were extensions of my own body. He who is forced to live as I do, without having consented to this life, frequently escapes by wandering around and about and therefore places the highest value on shoes. I could say that my shoes are the best thing about me, but all I do is think that thought. My commentary on the remaining shoes, which strike me as poorly cut, is short. It's always the same thing: the shoes are too narrow, the seams are too stiff, the stitching is in the wrong places, what they gain in elegance they lose in comfort. Habedank runs his fingers over the shoes as I describe them. For a moment I have the impression that my efforts are meaningful and important. I don't know any other work where one individual's sensations (a surrogate for those of others) play such a decisive role. After I finish my commentary, Habedank opens his drawer and pulls out a checkbook. For every evaluation, the Weisshuhn Shoe Company pays me two hundred marks. That means that Habedank shoves a check for twelve hundred marks across his desk. Afterwards he reaches behind him and places four pairs of new shoes on the desktop. I can tell by their form which cutters they come from. I stow the shoes in my canvas bags. Now it can only be a matter of seconds before Habedank asks me to join him for a cup of coffee. Then we'll talk about electric trains from the 1950s.

Unfortunately the firm has to economize, he says instead.

I don't know what to say to that, and wait for his next sentence.

What I mean is, says Habedank, that in the future I'll only be able to pay you fifty marks per walking unit, in other words for every pair of shoes.

That seems rather drastic, I say.

The situation has changed.

So suddenly?

Yes, says Habedank, we now have some pretty powerful competition. The luxury market is doing very well, and others have caught on.

Aha, I say.

To make up for that, you'll be allowed to keep the shoes you test, says Habedank.

Now the office is quiet. Suddenly it dawns on me why Frau Fischedick and Herr Oppau never left the room. They wanted to hear how Habedank would say this—no, they wanted to see how I would take the demotion. But there's nothing to see. I only wonder if Habedank is really trying to tell me I might as well give up the job. But then why did he hand me four new pairs of shoes? Evidently the firm still values my future work, though only at a quarter of the old price, if I ignore the in-kind gift. But what am I supposed to do with all those new shoes? I'll have to either hoard them or give them away.

I'm sorry, says Habedank, the pay reduction wasn't my decision, I'm just supposed to tell you.

I nod. The truth is, I'm not really surprised. This is the kind of situation that has given rise to my sense of living without inner authorization. I've experienced them frequently. I don't even have any desire to repeat the words I've often thought following similar experiences, and which I could think again now. Misfortune is boring. I wait to see if Habedank will ask me to join him for a cup of coffee in the cafeteria. But today there is no invitation—evidently because Habedank has some degree of sympathy for my situation. He scrunches a piece of cellophane and drops it on his desktop. The crumpled ball slowly crackles back open. Just when I'd enjoy listening to the crackling, I stand up and say to Habedank: You'll have the new evaluations in about three weeks.

A minute later I'm waiting for the train that will take me home. A disabled man is buying a can of beer at a french fry stand. The man has no arms, only hands attached to his shoulders. Four steps away, two crows are trying to peck open a plastic bag full of garbage. Using his right shoulder-hand (or should I say hand-shoulder?), the disabled man presses the can against his neck and opens it with his teeth. The crows manage to open the plastic bag, immediately sending orange peels, yogurt cartons and pizza boxes flying around the train platform. The public display of misery is disgusting, but it gives expression to my own horror as well.

Is there a general decline or isn't there? I can see several valid arguments on both sides. I stare at the trash and decide: there is a general decline. I await the day when all living things will confess their embarrassment. A mother with a stroller appears at the foot of the stairs leading up to the train platform. The child is gnawing on a balloon with his sharp little teeth. The teeth slide off the rubber and make a kind of gnashing creak—a sound I couldn't stand just a few years ago. Then the train comes humming along. The mother with the stroller waits for me to open the doors to the car for her. I don't know how it happened that I'm no longer bothered by the sound of teeth rubbing against rubber. I see it as a sign of hope. Evidently some forms of opposition occasionally dissolve of their own accord. That could mean that I'm getting closer to the day when I will live *with* inner authorization. I retract my finding and come to a new conclusion: there is no general decline. I don't dare alert the mother to the potential fright that threatens her child should the balloon pop. An observation like that would have to be delivered both jokingly *and* admonishingly. But I can't find the right words to elegantly combine jest and warning and at the same time conceal my own anxiety. Just last night in bed, shortly before falling asleep, I knew I had two train tickets left in my wallet; I now remove the second one and insert it into the ticket validator. How carefully we prepare the ground for major misfortune! Presumably I'll have to give up the job with Weisshuhn. The humiliation of working for only a quarter of the old honorarium is too much even for a tolerant man like me. Presumably I won't be meeting Habedank anymore. I'll put the four pairs of shoes he gave me through the usual paces and send them back in the mail, together with the evaluations. At Ebert Platz I get off the train with the intention of quickly vanishing into Gutleut Strasse, when suddenly I see Regine heading my way. She holds out her hand and kisses my cheek. Regine is only a little younger than I am. I'm amazed at her youthfulness. She asks what I'm doing these days and I give an evasive answer, which she notices right away.

You don't have to pretend with me, she says.

Fine, I say.

You still don't want to tell me what you're up to?

I just lost a job, I say.

Oh, says Regine.

Years ago Regine and I both worked as interviewers; for a while we even worked together. I remember one afternoon when she spent a whole hour asking me all about facial tissues, and afterward I quizzed her on plastic suitcases. Unfortunately the agency did away with the long interviews and replaced them with street polls. We were expected to stand outside schools, department stores, and government offices and survey people about tax policy and TV guides. Neither of us wanted to do that, and so we went our separate ways.

Are you working these days? I ask.

I'm taking a course to be a death companion, says Regine.

Oh, I say, unable to suppress a laugh.

It's a serious matter, says Regine.

I'd like to ask her what they teach in such a course, but don't dare.

Is it going well? I ask instead.

Recently they wanted to send me out for the first time to accompany a woman who was ninety-one years old, but she sent me away after half an hour.

Now we both laugh, avoiding each other's eyes.

She probably thought you were death in person come to take her away, I say.

I didn't see it that way.

After all, someone who's dying resents everybody who's going on living, I say.

You talk, says Regine, as if you'd already died once.

Of course I have, many times, haven't you?

We laugh, and I don't know if Regine fully understands my last remark. She holds out her hand and says goodbye.

Give me a call, she says in parting.

I don't need a death companion, I want to call out after her, but at the last moment I hold my tongue.

A little later it occurs to me that Regine and I actually died once *together*. First I had interviewed her about vacations and long distance travel, then she interviewed me about canned food and ready-made dinners. After that we were completely exhausted and lay down on her carpet. We drank half a bottle of wine and goofed around until our eyelids started to droop. When we woke up we undressed and slept together. Then a strange thing happened. Regine was lying next to me, studying her naked torso. She'd turned quiet and sad, but it took me a while to catch on. She asked me to look at her breasts. That's all I've been doing the whole time, is what I think I replied. Well evidently you weren't paying enough attention, she said. What are you getting at? I asked. Didn't you notice that my nipples aren't doing what they're supposed to? Regine was proud of her big long nipples. During erotic interludes they would grow erect, which she always considered to be a sign of her vitality. Now they were bent to the side or folded over or pressed into her areolas. I had noticed the change but didn't think it meant anything. Only gradually did it dawn on me that Regine was physically distressed. I went so far as to say she shouldn't take her nipples so seriously. And at that point we first fell silent and then died together as a couple.

Inside my apartment I open the windows, lie down on the floor and switch on the TV. I catch a film about blue-footed boobies in the Galapagos Islands. These are large, white-feathered birds with blue feet. They resemble geese and move in a similarly clumsy manner. On the Galapagos

Islands they find ideal breeding grounds, says the speaker. The birds nest on the ground, the surrounding water is clean and rich in fish. The birds are called boobies because of how they have to move their luxurious bodies during the long run-up required for takeoff. The blue-footed boobies appeal to me; at the moment I'd like to be one myself. I wouldn't mind being called a booby on TV, either, since as a blue-footed booby I'd finally have nothing more to do with words and their meanings. Or perhaps the animals' amazing white bodies make me think of Margot's little white body. It could also be that running into Regine is to blame for my sudden desire for a woman. I turn off the TV. A button pops off my shirt and rolls a ways on the floor. I watch it until it flips over and stops moving. Through the walls I hear the children in the apartment next door calling each other *asshole* and *dumb jerk*. They must be more or less like the children that made Lisa sick. I'd like to call Lisa and ask her how she's doing, but I wouldn't like for Renate to pick up and for me to have to talk with her. I don't move, listening to *asshole*, *asshole* shouted next door. Among the new shoes Habedank gave me is a pair of barely affordable hand-welted loafers made of genuine kidskin. They feel fantastic. It's a little after 3 p.m. Presumably Margot doesn't have any customers now and is eating a bowl of soup in the middle sink. The cat will be curled up sleeping in the sink on the left. I leave the apartment and head to Margot's. She'll probably be surprised to see me again so soon. I follow a Japanese woman who's eating a peach as she walks. The peach is small, it fits the Japanese woman's hands, which are also small, and it fits her mouth, which is so small that it hardly even strikes you as a mouth. After a short while the peach is eaten up; the Japanese woman is holding the pit in her small hands. Or is it called a stone? If I'm not mistaken when I was little I used to call it a stone, but then I started calling it a pit more and more often. Or was it the other way around? Why did I change from stone to pit, when from today's perspective there was absolutely no need to do that? The Japanese woman wraps her peach pit in a tissue. I have to turn left, but because I want to see what the Japanese woman will do with the peach pit (stone), I act a little like I'm just loafing and looking around. O wondrous awe for that which is foreign! The Japanese lady doesn't have the courage to simply toss the peach pit (stone) onto the street or into some garden. She stashes what's left in her tiny purse, which could just as well be called a peach pit pursette. I'm only a few steps away from Margot's. I can't hide my excitement—a silent twitch in my knees gives it away. In the display window of Margot's salon, all three neon tubes are lit. I see the door open and out steps Himmelsbach. That wasn't supposed to happen. Himmelsbach walks off to the right, so he doesn't notice me. In one fell swoop it's clear I can't go see Margot now, too. I probably won't ever be able to again. I can't tell whether Himmelsbach had his hair cut or not. Quietly and fruitlessly I rail against the furtiveness of life. One corner later it occurs to me that without this furtiveness I would have been dead a long time ago. This contradiction leads me to a momentary insight into the stuff of my insanity. If you go crazy someday, I think, it will mean that you've finally been cut by these constantly opening and closing shears. Himmelsbach is wearing a dark slouch hat with a wide brim. Playing the artiste—what ridiculous affectation! Unfortunately I get jealous, right here on the street. At the same time I feel sorry for Himmelsbach. He looks more down and out than in recent days. For a while I follow him aimlessly. Maybe he'll off take his hat, then I'd know for certain. Under no circumstances is he allowed to see me. And I have no desire to talk with him either. I can't let him see that I'm brooding over him and Margot. The best thing would be if he sat down somewhere, took off his hat, and mulled and meditated for a bit. But Himmelsbach doesn't rest and doesn't mull: those are my habits, not his. His pants look as if he'd borrowed them. Himmelsbach reaches into his jacket pocket and takes out a few sunflower seeds. He breaks them one by one with his incisors, using his fingernails to extract the white kernels. Regrettably, I ask myself if Margot is a woman who augments her income with occasional prostitution. But to tell the truth, I don't want to think about problems at all. I've already done that too often in my life, I feel too old for it now. I look for some distraction. I'd like to at least wander around the embankment and look up at the occasional tree and observe the light among the leaves. But the embankment isn't readily available, so I have to content myself with ordinary neighborhood streets. Under no circumstances may I let things get to the point where the only time I find my life bearable is when I'm wandering around. From the way Himmelsbach is walking, I can't tell whether he's just slept with someone or not. For the time being I try to split myself into two people, into a sober rambler who's lost both his work and his woman on the same day, and an active dreamer who doesn't want to hear anything about that. The split succeeds, at least for a while. Already I'm struck by the strong smell of the linden blossoms that must be around here somewhere. Shortly after that a cockeyed dog comes up between two parked cars. I didn't know that cockeyed animals even existed. The dog trots up to me; I can no more look him in the eye than I could a cockeyed human. I'm very grateful to him for the distraction he's providing me. I'm also grateful to a schoolteacher, for the same reason. She's standing at a streetcar stop with a dozen children. Suddenly the teacher says to her pupils: Don't take up so much room, line up more economically! That remark immediately predisposes me against the teacher. I manage to work up an inner indignation such as I haven't had in a long time. Line up more economically, I mumble to myself, words like that are the foundation of misery. The teacher is treating the children like umbrellas or folding chairs that can be stowed here or stashed there as needed. Is it any wonder that people refuse to consent to life from childhood on? Then the split in my consciousness starts to wear off. The experiences I have disowned come back bit by bit. Now my rambling about is no more than a bizarre play of melancholy and numb rigidity. I admit it would be painful if I couldn't see Margot again. I curse her, but that doesn't help. Dear Margot, did you have to hurt me with Himmelsbach of all people? I remember a saying I used to think when I was sixteen years old about nurses, secretaries and hairdressers: Dumb girls fuck good. I didn't come up with it, I was only parroting it, at that time I had no idea about nurses, secretaries, hairdressers or any other women. I try to foist the memory of this saying onto my split doppelgänger, unfortunately without success. The saying only causes me to groan; no one else knows. What I'd like most of all is to go straight to Margot and tell her what an indescribable simpleton I was when I was sixteen. And now I've lost sight of Himmelsbach in the whole mess. I ask myself whether the moods that pass through me are part of my life or not. I'm so dazed and feeble that I run into a parked car with my right knee. I'm put off by two children who cross my path saying choc instead of chocolate. Could this be the beginning of insanity? All the same, I don't want to complain or admonish. Complaining and admonishing are the favorite occupations of ninety-five percent of humanity, and my conceit wants nothing to do with them. I only want to give brief expression to my daily damnation and then go on living. No, it's not the damnation; it's the day's peculiarity I want to get rid of. Just how is it possible that I'm longing for a hairdresser I've met at most a half dozen times and whom I hardly know beyond her first name, that I'm jealous of a photographer who's half on the skids, and that I'm mourning for a job that didn't keep me fed anyway, and all that on a single day? It seems to me I can't go home under the influence of this peculiarity. I sit down on a wooden bench and stare at the nearby brambles, which I admire because they convey nothing except their own enduring. I'd like to be like these brambles. They're there every day, they resist by not disappearing, they don't complain, don't speak, they don't need anything, they're practically invincible. I feel a yearning to take off my jacket and toss it in a high arc into the brambles. Perhaps that way I might connect with some part of their enduring strength. Even the word brambles impresses me. Maybe that is *the* word for the collective peculiarity of all life, the word I've been searching for all this time. The brambles express my pain without putting any strain on me. I look at the dusty tangle of their leaves, flecked with bird droppings that are either running down or have already hardened, I look at the many branches that have been knocked or torn off by children but persevere undiscouraged, and at the nerve-racking litter that collects around the roots but still doesn't diminish the shrub. When the daily peculiarity starts to get the better of me, I'll come here and toss my jacket into the brambles. I'd like to see the jacket lying among the branches as a sign. A completely clear image and still no one will recognize it. I'll stroll past my jacket whenever I want and be able to marvel at how it remains as invincible as the brambles, despite the fact that it grows older and less handsome with every new pain it absorbs. And I will admire the jacket as my surviving doppelgänger and so free myself from pain, at least for the time being. I can't fully rule out the possibility that I might be going crazy at *this* moment. What's clear in any case is that if I ever really throw my jacket into the brambles I will have gone crazy for sure. I haven't reached that point yet. I enjoy imagining a play-craziness designed to help me live unperturbed. Now and then the pretend craziness should pass over into a genuine one—just for a few moments—and amplify my distance from reality. Naturally I'd have to be able to return to the game at any time, as soon as the genuine craziness stopped. Presumably this will prove that people can only be happy if they can choose between pretend craziness and genuine craziness whenever they want. In any case I've frequently observed that people are naturally predisposed to mental illness. I'm surprised so few people admit that their normalcy is merely feigned. Even the family walking past me right now is collectively crazy. A husband, wife, and grandma are making fun of a child. The child is still a baby; he's sitting in his carriage and can't do a thing. He can't hold his head up, can't grab things, can't really open his mouth right, can't swallow. Every time the child can't do something (right now he's drooling), the husband, wife or grandma squeals with pleasure. They don't realize that the delight they take in the child is really mocking and crude, though if they looked they might see that the child's fleeting gaze is searching for a faraway refuge. Strangely, my observation of the family lets me find my way back to reality. Only the child sinks deeper into his carriage, one millimeter at a time. I close my jacket and head home. The crazy family walks away, giggling.

My apartment is sitting there quiet and clueless. I don't feel miserable when I enter the kitchen. The telephone rings, I won't pick up. I take off my jacket and cut a slice of bread. I very much like the way the bread tastes. I take off my glasses and rub my eyes. Just as I'm about to put them back on, my glasses slip out of my hand onto the stone tile of the floor. The edge of the left lens is chipped. I put on my glasses and look at myself in the mirror. It's instantly clear that I won't be getting any new glasses, and that the little chip will become a sign. I go to the telephone and pick up after all. It's Susanne.

I found a letter from you, she exclaims, that you wrote me eighteen years ago.

Eighteen years ago? I ask tonelessly.

Yes, she says, eighteen years ago in August this is how you addressed me: Dearest Susanne...

But we weren't involved eighteen years ago, were we?

No, says Susanne, at least nothing happened.

So what does the letter say? Is it embarrassing?

No, says Susanne, love is embarrassing for you, but not for me.

Her answer perplexes me; I say nothing.

Shall I read it to you?

No, I say, it's enough for me to read it later.

You'll soon have a chance to do that, says Susanne, because I want to invite you to a little dinner party I'm having for a few friends and colleagues.

Do I know them too?

One or two of them, says Susanne, for example Himmelsbach.

Oh God, I say, that old stuffed shirt.

You can't call him that, says Susanne, laughing. Someone I used to work with will be there, too. She's now a sales manager for an upscale retirement home, that must be a dreadful job.

Susanne lists who else is coming. As I listen to her I sink into a kind of internal numbness. I wonder whether I was with Susanne eighteen years ago or if I only wrote her letters. I can't remember.

Do you prefer red wine or white? Asks Susanne.

Red, I say.

Susanne repeats the time and date of the dinner several times. I write them both down on the edge of a newspaper. I'm sure that I don't want to read the letter I wrote her eighteen years ago. Now Susanne is talking about what she's going to cook. I listen to her and chew on my bread without making any noise. The taste of the rye softens the peculiarity of the fact that I will soon be sharing a table with Himmelsbach.

# 7

FOR SOME TIME NOW I'VE BEEN TRYING TO THINK WHAT
Susanne's apartment reminds me of. We're sitting at a large
oval table covered with a white damask tablecloth. The nap-
kins are also damask, so stiff and smooth that at first I had
trouble using them to wipe my mouth. For starters we had
artichoke salad with spinach and pine nuts, followed by
grilled scallops with prosciutto. Susanne is an excellent
cook, although I did get a little impatient when she went on
a tad too long about the provenance of pine nuts and species
of scallops. Prints by Miró and Magritte are hanging on the
wall to my left and right, respectively—both framed. Three
unused chairs have been moved along the left front wall of
the room and strewn with small silk pillows—probably just
so the guests can casually run their hands over the fabric.
Now I've got it; the apartment looks half like a lingerie store
and half like a box of chocolates from the 1970s. The glass-
fronted china cabinet is full of little dolls, porcelain animals,
old silverware, mementos and a pearl necklace. It could just
as well be candies, photographs, fine chocolates, silk ribbons
and decorative boxes. Half an hour ago I renamed the living
room Restaurante Margarita Mendoza, which delighted
Susanne. Since not everyone knew where the name
Margarita Mendoza came from, I explained about Susanne's
theatrical past. Telling the story made it seem embarrassing
to me, but probably no one noticed. Apparently Susanne
liked my presentation; afterwards she thanked me with a
hug. Now at least on this evening and in this room and for
these people she counts as an artist. Susanne rolls in a dain-
ty brass dessert cart—baked peaches with mascarpone. From
behind, Susanne bends over my shoulders; her thin, light

gray silk dress passes a gentle tremor from her body to mine. She's wearing high-heeled evening sandals made of kid-leather with decorative pink satin ribbons. I could hold a small lecture about her shoes that would astonish all the guests, but I decide not to, or maybe I will later. Apart from Susanne and Himmelsbach I don't know anyone here. Himmelsbach is hardly paying any attention to me. He's carrying on a lively conversation with the person sitting next to him, a tourist program director who admits in an amused voice that by now she's as devoid of ideas as the tourists she's supposed to motivate. For the second time she declares, a little too loudly, that she doesn't intend to carry on with that job much longer. The minute I look at Himmelsbach I feel a wave of involuntary reactions ripple through me. His hair doesn't appear to have been cut recently, but I can't say that with absolute certainty. For nearly fifteen minutes now, Himmelsbach's constant proximity has been making me feel slightly nauseous. It reminds me of an unpleasant experience I once had on a trip. About fifteen years ago, back when I still had a car, I drove to Abruzzo, down all the winding mountain roads. During the whole trip I was as nauseous as I am now, and up to the last switchback I didn't know whether the nausea would last or not, just like I don't know now. On my way here I wondered whether or not I ought to say anything meaningful. At the moment I feel both agitated and embarrassed—an unpleasant mix I'm well acquainted with. This often leads to a third thing, namely a mute, inner dryness that's hard for me to get out of my system. The woman sitting to my right (Susanne is on my left), Frau Balkhausen, is drooping a bit from fatigue. She's already spoken several times about her work as a customer service advisor in a luxury retirement home; that may be all she knows. Presumably she expects me to keep her entertained, but my inner dryness still won't let go. Frau Dornseif, the tourist program director, is complaining that the only men who flirt with her anymore are completely unacceptable. Her comment pleases me, since it's plainly aimed at Himmelsbach as well, but Himmelsbach ignores it and goes right on talking with Frau Dornseif. Susanne laughs.

Lately it's been getting downright scary! says Frau Dornseif. The only men I have anything to do with are old or sick or slobs or losers! It's horrible!

Frau Dornseif feels amused again, this time by her own complaint; Himmelsbach gazes into his glass.

Some day, I say to Frau Dornseif, you're going to get involved with one of those ugly men.

Never, says Frau Dornseif.

Just wait, I say, some day you'll stop resisting! People love when they no longer want to run away from the other person, even though they sense this other person is bound to make impossible demands.

Bravo! says Susanne.

How boring, says Frau Dornseif.

Boring lovers are the deepest and longest lasting, I say.

My God, says Frau Dornseif.

What was that about love, says Susanne, can you say it again?

People love, I repeat, when they're no longer running away, even though they sense that they'll be facing impossible conditions.

Demands, was what you said.

What?

. . . that the other person is bound to make impossible demands, says Susanne.

I wouldn't have thought that Susanne would be so taken with my definition of love, which doesn't strike me as all that remarkable. Everyone except Himmelsbach looks at me. My inner dryness forces me to swallow.

Could you explain that? asks Frau Balkhausen.

I take a breath and drain my glass.

People love, I say, when they realize that this particular love renders all their earlier views about love superfluous. Do you understand?

No, says Frau Dornseif.

I don't believe, say I, that you're actually content to detest the slobs and losers. You'd like not to detest them so severely, at least not all of them, not all the time. You'd like to find at least one you don't detest, and once you've found him and are able to love him, then you'll also love your guilt, even more than—

What? Frau Dornseif cuts me off. Now I don't understand a thing, what does love have to do with guilt?

Because the person you now love came out of the multitude of those you previously rejected, and because you feel guilty about this unjustified rejection, I say.

Herr Auheimer, a lawyer who works in the same office as Susanne, raises his index finger and asks: Do you mean guilt in a justiciable sense or do you mean our collective guilt from original sin?

I don't care what kind of guilt you call it, I answer, at any rate I'm talking about the guilt that accumulates without being seen when we think we are living guiltlessly.

And what exactly is the origin of this guilt? asks Herr Auheimer.

Every person alive, I say, passes sentences on all those who live alongside him, often going on for decades condemning them. Then one day it dawns on us, and I mean every one of us, that we've been judging everybody else. The guilt that is unleashed by this insight benefits the one guilty person we are at last able to love. And there we have it: we love our guilt.

Susanne's eyes are sparkling. She thinks it's wonderful that a conversation like this is taking place at her living room table. I don't know if she realizes that I'm only talking this way because of her; I don't think she does.

But most people don't have the slightest inkling about this guilt, says Herr Auheimer. They consider themselves absolutely innocent.

That's the bad thing, I say, that's why it would be best if the universities finally started offering courses in Comparative Guilt Studies.

What? asks Frau Dornseif.

Comparative Guilt Studies, I repeat.

I've never heard of that, says Herr Auheimer.

You couldn't have, because it doesn't exist, or at least not yet, I say.

Susanne gets up, goes into the kitchen, and brings in a few more bowls of baked peaches and mascarpone.

But I don't want to keep talking the whole evening! I say.

Oh please, go on! Susanne calls out.

Susanne refills my wine glass and turns to face me as she sits down.

Do you understand Comparative Guilt Studies as a historical investigation? asks Herr Auheimer.

Among other things, I say. We all live in systems that are not of our own making. We can't do anything about these systems; they alienate us. They alienate us because we notice that over time we gradually assume their guilt. The fascist system produces a fascistic guilt, the communist system produces a communist guilt, the capitalist system produces capitalist guilt.

Aha! exclaims Herr Auheimer, now I understand! You're saying that guilt arises when people change systems?!

Most people don't get that far at all, I say with pointless exactitude—just like with love! I'm talking about the ordinary guilt of these systems that slowly migrates inside us, as we believe we are living guiltlessly within these systems. *All* political systems want the same thing, namely the elimination of unhappiness. And that's exactly why all these movements have more to do with fantasy than politics, you understand? Because the elimination of unhappiness is something no one can really want.

And where does that leave the guilt? asks Herr Auheimer.

The guilt, I say, comes from the fact that we all know this to be true in principle, but nevertheless we let ourselves be taken in by people who convince us to believe in life without unhappiness.

I get it! exclaims Frau Dornseif. So that's what you mean!

Suddenly the whole table is talking about what they used to believe and how that made them guilty. Himmelsbach talks about believing mothers, fathers and teachers, Frau Balkhausen talks about her lapsed faith in universities, hospitals, and courts, Frau Dornseif about her belief in youth and men. I'm curious to know what guilt Susanne will mention, but she doesn't say anything. I have the feeling that Susanne would like most of all to send her guests home, because she no longer wishes to share in the evening commotion. Then she brings two new bottles of wine from the kitchen; I uncork them and refill the glasses. Frau Balkhausen and Frau Dornseif have the impression (if I'm not mistaken) that they're witnessing a kind of disclosure. At last they know that there's a man in Susanne's life, lurking backstage. Susanne and I play along, though neither of us knows if it really is a game and/or if we should sigh at our old act, or possibly giggle. Frau Balkhausen shyly asks me what profession I'm in. Her question snaps me out of my mood to some extent, as it reminds me that even on an evening like this my life remains unauthorized. But I chase away the sour note and answer, somewhat drunk and snorting, that I run an Institute for the Art of Memory and Experience.

Oh, says Frau Balkhausen, that sounds interesting.

I refill her wineglass, and I'm already beginning to

regret my joke when Frau Balkhausen asks what kind of people I deal with at the Institute.

The people who come to us, I answer, a little hesitantly and at the same time as if it were routine, are people who sense that their lives have become nothing more than one long drawn-out rainy day, and that their bodies are no more than the umbrella for this day.

And you help these people, right? asks Frau Balkhausen.

Well, yes, I hope I help them.

And how? I mean, what do you actually do?

We try, I say, to help these people rediscover experiences that have something to do with them, beyond all the TVs, vacations, highways and supermarkets, you understand?

Frau Balkhausen nods earnestly and examines the yellow silk rose beside her wine glass. The conversation is beginning to make me uncomfortable. It doesn't escape me that Frau Balkhausen seems to be interested in the kind of experiential aid I am offering, and that she's about to ask more questions. Before she can get to them, however, I stand up and take a few aimless steps around the room. In the meantime I say goodbye to Herr Auheimer, who thanks me for my "clear-sighted remarks" (his very words) and then leaves. In a few minutes it will be 11 p.m. I hang around the door to the kitchen because Susanne and I agreed that at the end of the evening she'd give me the letter I wrote her eighteen years ago. But things turn out differently. Just when I'm right in front of the kitchen door Himmelsbach sidles up to me and asks if he might speak with me for two minutes about a personal matter. I cringe, since I can't imagine what kind of personal matter might tie me to Himmelsbach, and I'm afraid that someone like him might actually try to put whatever anonymous-personal thing it is into words. But I can't dodge him. He backs me against the wardrobe and then says in an appropriately quiet voice: I'd like to ask you a favor.

I give Himmelsbach a look that is clearly puzzled and

probably unsympathetic, but he refuses to be scared off—
on the contrary, he even considers my look to be encouraging.

You once wrote for the Gazette, he begins.

My God, I sigh, that was an eternity ago!

I know, says Himmelsbach.

I was still a student back then!

Yes, said Himmelsbach, but you know who's in charge there.

I don't think so.

Of course you do, Himmelsbach insists, for example you know Messerschmidt.

Don't tell me he's still there! I exclaim.

Why not? Himmelsbach asks. Are you saying you can't stand him?

What do you mean can't stand him, I answer, I just can't get anywhere with him, his need to classify things, his penchant for platitudes.

But you know him?

Only from back then, I say.

So you don't have anything more to do with the Gazette? asks Himmelsbach.

All of a sudden I sense what he's after.

You know, I say, those provincial papers always attract a lot of people with half or a quarter or even an eighth of a talent—not a pleasant mix. And the smaller the talent, the more wildly it's wielded by the person in question. I don't want to be seen there, if you get what I mean.

I can't afford to be as picky as you, says Himmelsbach, at least not every day.

He gives a short, mocking laugh, which makes me like him for a moment, just as in the old days. That's probably why I devote half a minute to making his life a little easier.

You want to take pictures for Messerschmidt, and I'm supposed to inquire if he could use you?

Exactly, says Himmelsbach.

And why don't you ask him yourself?

I'm too old for defeats, says Himmelsbach.

And if it doesn't work out?

Then I won't find out directly, just from you. The cushion would allow me to withstand the defeat.

I like his explanation: my silence expresses my general consent. Himmelsbach moves me. Evidently he (like Susanne) is convinced of my importance/subtlety/significance—what's more, he credits me with influence in the city.

Fine, I say, I'll give Messerschmidt a call.

Mmm, says Himmelsbach, I'll never forget it.

Let's wait and see.

And now? What should we do now? Susanne calls out and heads our way.

I'm going to the Orlando for a while, says Himmelsbach.

Good idea, let's go to the Orlando!

After a few sighs the prevailing view is that a visit to the Orlando discotheque would be a great way to top off the evening. I whisper in Susanne's ear that the Orlando doesn't do anything for me and I'd rather go home.

Come on, says Susanne, don't be a party pooper, and she kisses me on the ear.

I'd better not! Because if I did go then I'd really be a party pooper.

Frau Balkhausen is looking for her purse; Susanne laughs.

The night is young, says Frau Dornseif, the music in the Orlando will catapult us into the weekend like a, like a, my God, she says, I can't think of a thing.

Himmelsbach checks that his coin purse is properly seated in his pants pocket and shakes my hand. I make sure we don't go down the stairs together. I notice that Frau Balkhausen would gladly talk with me some more—even in a disco if necessary. I offer to help Susanne clean up. Frau Balkhausen realizes she's being given the brush-off and disappears. Two minutes later, I say goodbye myself. Despite his head start, I'm only some twenty-five meters behind Himmelsbach. I notice that he's filled his left pants pocket with peanuts, which he takes out one by one and chews as he walks.

Four days later, on a Saturday morning, I am making my debut as a vendor at the flea market, standing behind the trestle table that Lisa left behind in the basement. I've tacked a sheet of thin white paper onto the tabletop, and laid out the shoes I recently received from Habedank, all in a row. I'm asking eighty marks for each pair—a ridiculous price. There's a constant stream of market-goers passing by, but hardly anyone is interested in my wares. They look at me and not at the shoes. I've been here nearly two hours and have yet to be asked what the shoes cost. To my left is a man who deals in militaria; he isn't selling anything either. He's set up a portable TV and is watching a documentary on Thuringia. The dealer to my right is wearing a Mickey Mouse tie; he specializes in cheap metal toys. Actually he's no more a dealer than the man with militaria is or I am. We stand around, glancing now at the sky, now at the ground, now at the TV. I keep asking myself which feeling is stronger: futility or pointlessness. It's a question I can't answer. So I quickly skip to the next question: which will come for me first, insanity or death? The mere mention of the word death intimidates me, and I drop that question right away. But what else should I think about? I sense that my attempt to be a dealer in luxury shoes may be my last chance to find a so-called normal life. I observe the people passing by and tell myself that I'm like they are. I list what I have in common with them. That goes pretty well, for a while. But then I realize that I can make whatever list I want and the details still won't all add up. Nor do they have to add

up simply because life progresses, hence there is no reason for me to approve the sum total, even on this late morning. I don't even know how today's peculiar tryout as a flea market vendor is supposed to square with the rest of my life. I think about the letter I wrote Susanne eighteen years ago and which I read once again a few days back. It's an embarrassing document of a youthful passion that began with great promise and suddenly fizzled out. What's even more unpleasant is that I've forgotten the dalliance, which Susanne fortunately doesn't hold against me. I'm almost certain we won't fail to come together this time. What isn't clear to me, however, is whether I ought to acquaint Susanne with the meaning of the leaf room when she comes to visit. Certainly I won't have to strain myself to get the concept across to her. It's just a little silly that my own interest in the leaves has fallen off substantially during the last few days. They've turned parchment-like and brittle in the dry air of the apartment. Just yesterday I was holding a bunch of them in my hand; their edges were already crumbling away. I gave up walking through the room with my feet slanted and scuffing up little piles with my shoes. I won't be bringing any more leaves into the apartment, either. I'm more likely to dissolve the leaf room in its infancy. I look down the little slope that drops away behind the stalls. The slope functions as a kind of garbage dump, where the vendors toss whatever they no longer need: plastic bags, tarps, metal buckets, beer cans, cardboard boxes, clothes, construction rubble, debris. I like the word debris. It expresses the peculiarity of life every bit as well as the word brambles. Presumably even a little better, because the mustiness of all life resonates better in debris than in brambles. I no longer know what to distract myself with. The militaria dealer to my left is watching the news on his portable TV. A politician is being interviewed. As usual he is surrounded by a number of pompous pundits who gaze into the camera with serious faces. It may still be possible for me to become a background man like that. Whenever politicians appear on TV, I would show up and act as a stage prop. I have an impeccably serious face that's excellently suited for underscoring any and every point. I'll have a lot to do; I'll earn money. TV background man—that could be my dream job. At last I'll be allowed to keep silent and even get paid for doing so. Although I'm just conjuring these ideas for my personal entertainment, I wonder if I really shouldn't call a TV station and offer my services. A knit glove on the ground helps me chase away my little delusion. Earlier the glove was lying on a gigantic bargain table diagonally across from me. Then someone brushed against the edge of the table, shoving the glove into the abyss. Now it's lying in the dust, while deep inside me it is turning into a sign of persistence and steadfastness that will outlive all times and flea markets. It's almost noon. I'm not selling anything; it seems to me as though I were dead. You can tell from looking at the people streaming by that they're all thinking the same thing: What happened in this man's life that he's now selling shoes? I examine my jacket, which I've draped over an iron railing, but nothing comes of it. It would be better if I went home, but then I'd have to grapple with the thought of having failed. Finally I manage to muster some interest in the young people, who feel a fivefold compulsion to express their youth: 1) through their fidgeting, 2) through the objects (cola, popcorn, comics, CDs) in their hands, 3) through their dress, 4) through their music, as seen in the plugs in their ears and the wires around their necks, and 5) through their slang. The next time I'm with Susanne I'll have to tell her about this hyperreality. She'll laugh, and we'll both be glad that at least we're no longer young. A quiet man between forty and forty-five steps up to my table and looks at the shoes. He picks up the pair on the far left, puts his hands inside and stretches the soles by bending the toe towards the

84

heel. I wonder whether I ought to offer a few words of explanation, but it's obvious that the man knows his shoes and would only consider explanations a nuisance. He tests two other pairs the same way. Then he kicks up his left leg and compares the size of the shoe he's holding with that of the one he's wearing. My shoes fit. A moment later he takes out his wallet and tells me he'd like to take the three pairs of shoes he just tested. I state the price and pack the shoes in two plastic bags. Seconds later the man places four bills in my hand in the exact amount of two hundred forty marks. Then he gives me a curt nod and walks on. It's obvious that after this remarkable success I will soon fold up my stand and go home. I only want to spend a few more moments experiencing the inner warmth that my joy is kindling inside me. I put the money away and lean back against the iron railing. I look at the trash and ask myself how the construction rubble and the debris got here. It's strange that I'm already beginning to feel at home in these chance surroundings. Hopefully my inner zeal doesn't mean I'm starting to fantasize about a career as a flea market vendor. My tendency to find quick comfort in the nearest pile of mortar is presumably left over from after the war. I was a child then, running around through the wreckage and asking at every ruin whether there was a place to stay. The war had just ended, but from the look of the destruction I was sure that a new war could break out at any moment and force everyone to stay in the next best dust-hole. No, I won't go home right away. First I'll drop by the Café Rosalia. I haven't been there in ages. I'll have a meal befitting the business of the day and go on abandoning myself to my joy. In four or five moves the table is folded up; the unsold shoes vanish inside two plastic bags. Lisa and I used to go to the Café Rosalia quite frequently; I hope it's still there. It's not a real café at all, rather a large bakery with two small dining rooms you reach through a narrow hall. These days the place seems utterly old fashioned. On the way there I pass a notions store with a wonderful bargain in the display window—a box full of countless black and white balls of knitting yarn, one mark apiece. An absolutely one-of-a-kind sight! If Lisa were there I'd walk in and buy one roll of the black yarn and one roll of the white and place them on a shelf at home and gaze lovingly upon them as if they were living creatures. Thank God, the Rosalia's still there! And it still has a single small coat tree. That means that most of the guests crumple up their jackets and capes and bags and purses and stack them on top of each other on the chairs next to them. All these weird, mostly dark-colored lumps and tangles look like small shrouded creatures, so that for a moment the whole place looks like a café for animals. The Rosalia is a popular place; the only available seats are along the back wall, by the courtyard. At the table on my left two older ladies are sitting with a boy who's about nine years old; an elderly couple is on my right. I lean my bags against the wall and order prix fixe no. 1—salmon with rice and spinach. The tablecloth has been carefully tucked in at three points, presumably by an abiding grandmother who's never seen in the guest rooms. The boy is spooning blueberries and milk from a glass bowl. He squashes many of the berries, making the milk bluer and bluer. Milk blue—is there such a color? Probably not, but it glows all the way over to where I'm sitting. The woman next to the boy complains about the size of the strawberries on her cake. The boy reprimands her: does she have to find fault with everything—even the strawberries? The elderly husband to my right also gets criticized. Don't keep looking at your broken watch, says the woman next to him. The boy has eaten the blueberries and is leaning forward. Do you have to drag your hair all over the table, says the woman the boy had just criticized. I understand that my good fortune consists in not having anyone who complains about me. The boy crawls underneath the table. He lies down on his back and looks at the table from below. Do you have to wipe the floor with your new shirt, the other woman calls out under the table. As if there weren't enough evidence already that the world is an impossible place to put up with, here's one more proof. At least the salmon is excellent, as is the spinach. I try to wink at the boy under the table, but it doesn't work. The women notice my solidarity with the boy and consider it problematic or possibly inappropriate. They tell the boy to get up. Now he's sitting quietly between the two women. Meanwhile they look at me like a corrupter of children who's just been unmasked and warded off in the nick of time. At last I, too, want nothing more, and merely observe the relentlessly reprimanded world.

# 8

MESSERSCHMIDT SOUNDED FRIENDLY OVER THE PHONE, even affectionate. He acted as if he'd been waiting years for me to call. Apart from that he was so talkative that I hardly got a word in, though I didn't particularly mind that. He reminisced about our student years, and I was amazed at the profusion and precision of the details he had retained. Since I didn't have to say much, I was able to gently cover up the fact that our student years were a lot more discomfiting for me than for him. It took ten minutes before I could bring up the reason for my call. By then he'd already invited me twice to stop by his office. I had no need to visit the Gazette. I would have preferred to meet Messerschmidt in a café, but I was no match for his bubbly insistence. Towards the end of the conversation I managed to blurt out that I wasn't calling on my own account.

So, he shouted into the receiver, what is it then?

It's about, I said, it's about Himmelsbach, the photographer.

Oh God, said Messerschmidt.

What's the matter with him?

Himmelsbach seems to be a tragic character. No, on second thought he's not—he's just incompetent, said Messerschmidt.

You mean he's worked for the Gazette before?

He wanted to, said Messerschmidt, but it never happened. Once he overslept his appointment, another time he brought some pictures that were pretty bad, and I mean bad—not even fit for the Gazette! Messerschmidt said and gave a little laugh. On the third try his camera misfired and the fourth time he got into an argument with the presenters or something like that: in any case nothing with Himmelsbach ever worked out.

I see, I said, and then was silent. Actually I was already wondering how to tell Himmelsbach about the result of my intercession—no, actually I was annoyed because Himmelsbach hadn't told me the whole story—no, even more actually I immediately understood why he couldn't possibly tell me *that* whole story.

But why are we going on so much about Himmelsbach! said Messerschmidt. Don't you want to drop by some afternoon for coffee, why don't we say the day after tomorrow, that's Thursday, I'll just be sitting around and would love to see you.

Today is that Thursday, and I'm on my way to the Gazette. I'm even a little curious to see what Messerschmidt looks like. Back when we were young we used to see each other almost every day, and I have a clear recollection of feeling a little embarrassed for him. He was the leader of some Regional Committee for the Communist Party of Germany, meaning that he wrote, printed, and distributed leaflets outside the gates of large factories and agitated among the workers. When Mao died, he organized a spontaneous demonstration in the city. This consisted of a handful of men whose leader, Messerschmidt, carried a megaphone in his left hand and a fruit crate in his right. Every now and then he would climb up on the fruit crate, hold the megaphone to his mouth, and speak. With great sadness the Central Committee informs you that Comrade Mao Tse-Tung died last night at the age of eighty-two. It was amazing how Messerschmidt did this, as if it were the most natural thing in the world, as if his entire audience had always been or would soon become Chinese. To this day I remember his most unbelievable sentence: We will transform our sadness over the death of the Great Leader into energy. At the time I seriously wanted to ask Messerschmidt to teach me exactly how to perform this transformation, but those kinds of proclamations were precisely the reason we started growing further and further apart, until Messerschmidt resurfaced many years later in the editorial office of the Gazette and asked me on as an independent contributor. If Messerschmidt had realized that my memory is at least as good as his, he might not have invited me to stop by today. Naturally I'll only remind him of what I presume he wants to be reminded of. The Gazette's small office building is located behind two large department store warehouses. Cats prowl among the empty boxes in search of food. I watch them for a while; I like them a lot. I falter just outside the entrance and am about to head back home when a well-dressed man walks out of the newspaper building. The man has rolled up a copy of the Gazette into a small baton, which he strikes against his right thigh as he walks. I feel pressured by his bearing. It's peculiar, but from this moment on I know that there's no going back. For a moment the possibility flashes by that my inner reserves may be exhausted and obsolete. Immediately I'd like to know if there's such a thing as spoiled sensitivity or not, and if there is, whether spoiled sensitivity is itself a product of spoiled sensitivity and by what process sensitivity can be transformed into spoiled sensitivity. Maybe Messerschmidt knows, I think, quietly savoring my scorn. Seconds later I enter the main lobby of the newspaper. Some of my uneasiness subsides when I see that the advertisement office is still to the left of the main lobby. The editorial office is still on the second floor. On the stairs I run into the features editor Schmalkalde, who doesn't recognize me. Nineteen years ago he spent a year collecting all the brochures that anonymous distributors placed in his mailbox. He wanted to use the material to create a "Critical Primer on Communication," but it wound up never being printed. Now Schmalkalde walks past me like an unpublished book, staring at the floor. When I open the door to his office, Messerschmidt is cutting a peach with a small pocketknife. He puts down the pocketknife and comes up to me. He's plumped out and has a few fresh red spots on his face, as if he'd just been disgusted by something.

Hey! You're wearing yellow shoes! he exclaims. You know who always wore yellow shoes? Hitler and Trotsky—dictators wear yellow shoes, my friend.

I decline to comment and sit down. Messerschmidt walks around me and turns on the coffeemaker.

How are you? What are you up to? we ask each other.

I evade the question and say only that I'm struggling along somehow.

So, says Messerschmidt.

And you, are you doing well?

I'm doing great, says Messerschmidt. I can hardly believe how well I'm doing, my life strikes me as completely incredible.

The coffeemaker coughs and sputters, black coffee drips into the glass pot. Messerschmidt rinses two cups in a tiny sink and wipes them dry.

You know, don't you, he said, what a horrible pair of life-inhibitors my parents were, right? I'm sure I told you.

Didn't your father make your mother use his old underwear first as a dust rag and then for polishing shoes?

Man! What a memory! That's exactly right! Messerschmidt shouts. My whole childhood I had the feeling I had to rescue myself, no matter where or how. And can you believe that it wasn't until recent years that this feeling finally faded away? I'm a little baffled by the sheer fact that I managed to save myself. I'm living an utterly secluded life. Because I managed to save myself, I can't tolerate any noise. And because I'm afraid of people who always talk big, I don't like going to anything cultural. What I need is peace and quiet, and that's what I've found here with the Gazette.

Messerschmidt pours the coffee and chuckles to himself.

He still has the same old compulsion to confess; he talks the way he always did.

And you! he exclaims.

And me, I say, a little stupidly.

I'll never forget, says Messerschmidt, the way you analyzed the film *Casablanca* about eighteen years ago. Remember?

I shake my head.

The film makes such a strong impression, you said, says Messerschmidt, because the hero makes so many decisions that have far-reaching consequences. He leaves people and countries, he changes identities, women and political convictions. But the people who watch the film never make anything but small decisions, which have no consequences whatsoever. The most they ask themselves is whether they need a new TV or a new coat, that's all they have going on. In other words, says Messerschmidt, as far the people sitting in the movie house are concerned, everything in their lives has already been decided.

Did I say that? I ask.

That's what you said back then, says Messerschmidt, I still remember where, too, in the pizzeria at Adenauer Platz, it's not there anymore, remember?

I look Messerschmidt in the eye and don't remember.

The lie of *Casablanca*, you said, says Messerschmidt, is that it mixes a world of real-life decisions with the moviegoers' world of non-decisions to the point that the people watching the film delude themselves into thinking that their lives, too, are full of vital decisions.

Did I say that?

You put it so well it was fit to print, says Messerschmidt, and then you added that actually the film itself wasn't such a lie—just the way people used it, but that was precisely why the film was a lie, because it enabled the viewers to make it into one.

That sounds pretty good for back then, I say.

You mean you wouldn't judge it the same way now? asks Messerschmidt.

I would, I say, except I'd add that the film also enables a few delusions on the part of the interpreter.

We laugh.

You see! says Messerschmidt. You want some more coffee?

No thanks.

I hold my hand over my empty cup. The triumphant way in which Messerschmidt remembers me makes me embarrassed. At the same time I sense that far greater embarrassments are lying in wait. Messerschmidt picks up the peach he had set aside and cuts it into pieces. He takes a fork out of his desk drawer and jabs it into each tiny piece before putting it into his mouth. I'm already afraid he's going to give me a fork too and ask me to join in.

Don't you want to work for me again? asks Messerschmidt. After all, it worked out so well before between us?! I don't know what you're doing these days, but if you want to, as I said, says Messerschmidt.

I'm not sure I can answer that today, I say, simply because I don't want to turn down his offer right away.

Aha! says Messerschmidt. Is this modesty genuine or feigned?

The fact that Messerschmidt is pondering my modesty brings out my conceit. At the same time, he doesn't realize I only feel good if there's something I can conceal in every situation. Presumably this is due to a mechanism that continues to astound me, namely the way that people form new identities whenever someone comes too close. It's possible that my pensive nature will put an end to my relationship with Messerschmidt. In the meantime I've gone silent; I stare first at the edge of the desk, then at the remainder of the peach. Presumably Messerschmidt interprets my silence as serious consideration of his offer.

You can think it over, says Messerschmidt, all you have to do is call.

And there's nothing more to say about Himmelsbach? I ask.

I hope I'm not causing you any trouble, but I don't really want to have anything more to do with Himmelsbach.

All right, I say.

On my way home, I'm already feeling less certain that I'll decline Messerschmidt's offer. Even though I urgently need the money I can/could earn at the Gazette, I'm not so much thinking about myself as about Susanne. Susanne will overrate the newspaper world and finally feel that she's an important person. Some office workers walking behind me are talking in unpleasantly loud voices. I duck into the entranceway of an apartment house and let them pass. Now I'm walking behind a man whose left leg is a shade shorter than his right. With every step the left half of his body dips a little, which makes his gait look paddle-like. This paddle-like gait is just right for me at the moment, I think, and I go for a while imitating the man's walk. Shortly before I reach the bridge I run into Anushka, whom I spent some time courting thirteen years ago until she rejected me with the words: I'm far too bony for you anyway. With a brusque movement (she tilts her face, showing me her dismissively smooth left cheek) she lets me know that she doesn't wish to be stopped or spoken to. I understand her request and comply. I nod as I walk past her and repeat her words from back then to myself: I'm far too bony for you anyway. How peculiar that a single sentence should be the last thing I'm left with from Anushka. I'd like to talk with her right now about this particular peculiarity, though I'm sure she's forgotten what she said back then or else she never retained it, and besides I've known for a very long time now that the only way I can express life's peculiarity is by tossing my jacket into some brambles or debris. The man with the paddle-like gait takes a candy out of his pocket, discards the paper wrapper and pops the candy into his mouth. The wrapper sails onto the street where it makes a nice soft noise on the cement as I pass. I'd like to stop and listen to the crinkle of the candy wrapper for a few more seconds. As the peculiarity of Anushka's last sentence dissolves into the crinkle of the candy wrapper, I'd like to rename the collective peculiarity of all life *crinkle*. Most of all I'd like to bend down close to the wrapper, which is being blown back and forth by the wind. But I'd also like to go on following the man with the paddle-like gait a while longer, now almost in gratitude, since I have him to thank for my new word for peculiarity. As an experiment I imagine accepting Messerschmidt's offer. Overnight I'll become surrounded by a large assemblage of pompous local pundits, day in and day out. A little gloomy melancholy flies up to me, and I carry it with me across the bridge. An equally small pain clowns around inside me, saying: You need to look for what you stand to gain, and accept the offer. I can cope with the pain, but I have to do something about the melancholy. It's prancing in front of me, eager to start something with me. I name it Gertrude, so it's easier for me to ridicule. Gertrude Gloom, get lost. She immediately introduces herself: Hello, my name is Gertrude Gloom, may I be so bold as to take you down a peg? Get lost, I repeat. She refuses to leave, on the contrary, she grabs hold of me, I can feel her black warmth. Presumably she thinks that she has me in her grip. She forces me to the railing; I look down at the dark water. How about a separation from life, she asks, due to demonstrated lack of significance? I know these questions, they render me speechless. Gertrude talks to me the way you would to a recalcitrant child. Nevertheless, she's a bit annoyed because I again refuse to do everything she demands. For half a minute I struggle on the bridge with Gertrude Gloom, and then I notice that it's her strength that's starting to ebb, not mine.

Unfortunately, during my fight with Gertrude I've lost sight of the man with the paddle-like gait. A glass delivery truck slowly drives by, with two tall display windowpanes mounted on a frame in the flatbed. I wish that those two windowpanes would burst into pieces in my stead and fall right onto the street. But then I feel that such extreme wishes are no longer necessary. Gertrude Gloom has been overpowered, at least this time. If no other highwaymen are lying in wait, I'll soon be home. But my joy proves premature. On the other side of the bridge, Frau Balkhausen breaks away from a pack of pedestrians and heads straight for me. She holds out her small cold hand and looks at me.

The weekend is coming, she says, and I have no idea what to do.

Unfortunately I don't dare tell Frau Balkhausen that I'm feeling a bit debilitated after having just brought down Gertrude Gloom, and that I've long been indifferent to weekends, my own as well as those of others.

All I do is clear my throat.

I keep wondering what I might do, says Frau Balkhausen, but I'm not getting anywhere. I look out of the window and don't see a thing or else I see the same thing I saw yesterday and the day before. Perhaps you could advise me?

Me? I ask.

Don't you run an Institute for Memory Arts or Life Joy or something like that? You offer day courses, right? You told me so yourself. I'd be very interested in a course like that, I'm almost certain that you could help me.

I stare at Frau Balkhausen, probably too long. I'm moved and overcome with sympathy, for the moment I'm at a loss for how to respond and nonetheless I feel obligated. As it is, Frau Balkhausen did confide somewhat in me; I can scarcely resist her disclosure.

In that case why don't you call me, I say, how about Friday afternoon?

Gladly! Thank you!

Frau Balkhausen nods repeatedly; I give her my phone number, which she jots down on a matchbook.

Thanks very much, she says, thank you, and goes on her way.

I watch her as she goes; she doesn't turn around. She steps around a Turkish man who with his veiled wife is taking plastic clothes hangers from a large carton. I look at the Turkish couple with a hint of gratitude. The sight of them strengthens my feeling that I am once again moving in a world of reality situated far closer to earth than my own sphere of complications. That's probably why I've already forgotten about Frau Balkhausen. Five minutes later I'm home. Lately it's been happening more and more often that when I unlock the door to my apartment I think of my mother—about how she used to come home when I was a child and I would jump on her from the depths of our apartment. And how she would then sigh and tell me to let her come home first. And how I was a little upset by the fact that she wasn't in as good a mood as I was. Now I step into the entrance hall of the apartment and quietly say the same words my mother used to say back then: Let me come home first! And then I check to see whether I'm not sulking around somewhere as an indignant child. For a few moments I am both my mother and her child. Then I think that a person coming home is nothing more than a person coming home. It's so strange that I have to open the kitchen window. On the table there's a piece of bread that I wanted to throw away yesterday. Even while I'm slowly chewing away at the bread I'm a little indignant, just like an eight-year-old, and at the same time a little annoyed, just like his forty-eight-year-old mother. Shortly afterward I fall into an amazingly well-mannered mood. I close the window and step over to the telephone. I call Messerschmidt and tell him that I accept his offer.

# 9

THE PROBLEM IS THAT I DON'T KNOW ANY RESTAURANTS TO speak of, pleasant or unpleasant, expensive or cheap, German or foreign. Going out was not something Lisa and I did in the years we were together. Now I am supposed to/have to find a restaurant that's friendly and good and not too pricey. Susanne called this afternoon and said she'd like to go out to dinner. She asked me to pick her up at work. Naturally I didn't tell her that I don't have a clue about the restaurant scene; she probably wouldn't have believed me anyway. Even though I left early I have yet to find a suitable restaurant that I can casually suggest to Susanne. What I am finding is that I'm not enjoying this assignment one bit; on the contrary, there's hardly anything I could care less about than restaurants. Nevertheless I'm taking a second look inside an Italian restaurant called VERDI, which seems fine to me, if I ignore the name. I actually know a Greek restaurant close to the VERDI called MYKONOS, but that's out of the question because of the loud canned music. What are the criteria for choosing a restaurant? For me a place is basically acceptable if it isn't too crowded; I'm even prepared to put up with a less-than-excellent meal in return. Presumably Susanne has a different approach. I open the door of a Thai restaurant and am immediately struck by a sweetish, cling-clanging music. Good God! The low evening sun colors all faces yellow. I take a liking to a small group of children boasting about imaginary experiences. Even at their age they're talking fast and furious to ward off disappointment! On a side street a mother is sitting in a car nursing her baby. Women who have lost their figures flit past in broadly-cut dresses. A man pulls two sky-blue aluminum crutches out of a car and hobbles off. I think briefly about Lisa. It seems that I've forgotten her. No, that's not true. On the contrary, I think about her several times each day, but it no longer matters to me that I don't see her any more. How much time will it take before I can't recall her face and voice? I'm just about to peek inside the window of a Spanish restaurant when I notice Himmelsbach. Accompanied by Margot. So I was right! Himmelsbach is wearing his leather jacket, which is worn to the point of being slippery, and is chatting away at Margot. A camera is dangling from his neck. He's still dreaming his photographer dream and going on about that, using his index finger to point at the camera and occasionally taking it in his hand. The Spanish restaurant is called EL BURRO and looks tolerable, at least from the outside and at first glance. Now Himmelsbach and Margot are speaking at the same time and looking at the ground as they walk and talk. I get a little weak in the knees and feel the need to sit down. But I can't sit down at the moment; I have to keep an eye on Margot and Himmelsbach. Why do I get weak in the *knees*? I'd prefer to get weak in the head, since then I might be able to stop thinking. As it is, though, I ask myself how I ought to tell Himmelsbach that he won't get anywhere with the Gazette. And how should I dispel his suspicion that I had something to do with his rejection? I'll probably act as if I forgot what he asked me to do. Then he'd look at me like a lazy old loafer and no longer want to speak with me. I'd be happy with that. But then why do I feel guilty that nothing will become of Himmelsbach? Besides, it bothers me to sense this slight feeling of rivalry beginning to grow inside me. I think it's the first time that a woman whose trial was still pending, so to speak, was taken away from me or slipped through my fingers. Admittedly I didn't really show her much attention. I should have let Margot know that I was interested in her outside the salon as well. But the horrible truth is that I'm not really interested in her outside the salon. So then why does the sight of her cause me pain? And why don't I want her falling into the clutches of someone like Himmelsbach? A streetcar track cleaner comes jolting past, hissing and whistling, and stops my questions from pursuing me further. Himmelsbach drapes his right arm over Margot's shoulders as they walk and lets his hand hang down in front. I pick up my pace a little, because I want to see what Himmelsbach does with his hand and how Margot will react. It doesn't take long before Himmelsbach lets his hand swing in such a way that it occasionally brushes against Margot's bosom. And Margot doesn't wriggle out of his embrace. Apparently she doesn't mind being touched like that. This development has a positive effect on my sense of rivalry. Himmelsbach's adolescent antics suddenly make me feel sorry for him. The way he's touching Margot's bosom looks (is designed to look) as though it were happening inadvertently. Unbelievable! Himmelsbach is acting like a sixteen-year-old! He keeps stroking the tips of Margot's breasts as if by chance. That's exactly the approach I took with Judith when we were both seventeen. The intervals between contacts are getting shorter and shorter, to the point where for one moment his right hand is virtually grasping Margot's right breast and Margot seems neither shocked nor surprised by the advance. It's incredible! Himmelsbach, who is approximately forty-two years old, is resorting to the same moldy bag of adolescent tricks to put the moves on Margot, who's hardly any younger than he is.

This is why I end up making him into a grotesque figure in my mind. Now, if I'm not mistaken, giving up Margot won't be so difficult. In my thoughts a strange trade-off is taking place. Without intending to, Himmelsbach helped me find another job at the Gazette. To even things out I'm giving up a woman without a struggle. I'm using the pain incurred from losing Margot to absolve myself of any guilt due to my unsuccessful negotiation on Himmelsbach's behalf. Is that right? But I feel a further guilt because I am or will be lucky/successful with Messerschmidt myself. This bizarre guilt is both incomprehensible and terribly relentless. Of course there could also be an entirely different explanation (Possibility II): As a consequence of my guilt, Himmelsbach will never learn that he doesn't have any chance at the Gazette, therefore I transfer the guilt for my own success onto him as well, because where there was guilt on one occasion, new guilt will gather in the future. Possibility III seems very remote, though this may be mistaken: in actuality Himmelsbach and I have both long been searching for some physical contact, which was finally enabled through Margot's unsuspecting body. Because we both slept with her, we've come close to each other for the first time. Possibility IV, which makes me shudder the most, is that my hyper-proximity to Himmelsbach only proves that all life is nothing but one incessant mutual imposition, an unparalleled tangle of embarrassment. All of a sudden I go weak in the knees again. I've always said that my knees (to say nothing of my head) lack the strength needed to set these difficult problems straight. Fortunately I don't have my jacket on me. Otherwise the peculiarity of life, which is never overly kind to me, would force me to toss my jacket into some brambles or debris where I'd have to stare at it in silence for two hours. Fortunately during the course of this last deliberation I have lost sight of Himmelsbach and Margot. For a few moments I wonder whether I ought to leave town on account of Himmelsbach. The absurdity of this last thought makes me even weaker. The yellow sky is slowly taking on the color of oranges. I still have more than an hour before I'm scheduled to meet Susanne. Under no circumstance do I want to spend the entire time ruminating. It seems I have deceived myself. What's taking place inside me isn't a trade-off at all, but rather a gradual bowing down. Only what exactly is doing the bowing and what is making it bow? Good God, now these questions are starting up again. The sudden sight of a boy about ten years old comes to my aid. He steps onto the balcony of a building in a side-street and ties one end of a long string onto the balcony railing, while a clothes brush dangles down at the other end. He swings the brush back and forth for a while, then holds the string and waits until the brush has stopped moving. I sit on the sill of a display window and study the brush that is now slowly spinning around and around. The boy steps back inside the apartment and closes the balcony door. A little later his face appears in a side window, peering through the slit between the curtains. From there he watches the clothes brush, which is now at rest. I'd like to be as unruffled and balanced as a brush and then be watched benevolently by myself. A few seconds later I have to laugh at my previous sentence. At the same time I'm actually grateful to the sentence. It's merely a sign that I was able to calm myself. I even go so far as to think that some part of the brush's equilibrium has been passed to me. At the moment I'm no longer troubled by the fact that I don't understand everything. The orange-colored sky once again changes hues. A tint of old rose is moving over the ridge of the roofs, turning mauve somewhat higher up. A barely perceptible breeze rocks the brush back and forth. This purposeless rocking is also something I'd be happy to absorb. Now I consider not understanding everything a matter of dignity. After three quarters of an hour I have the feeling that the clothes brush is rocking back and forth inside my body.

Unfortunately Susanne didn't have time to spend the past hour close to a softly swaying clothes brush. She's jittery, drained, exhausted from the struggle. We go to VERDI. The food is supposed to be a sure bet; the place is almost full. The lighting has been dimmed, and luckily there isn't any music. For a while I watch the people constantly adjusting themselves, wiping their mouths, hitching up their pants

102

and skirts and fixing their hair. Susanne orders the chicken breast in tarragon-mustard sauce; I choose a sage-flavored focaccia. Susanne starts eyeing the people around us with suspicion, or else cursing them under her breath.

I can't stand the sight of any disgruntled faces today, says Susanne. All they do is make me angry and aggressive.

Susanne can't even bear the fact that the spoon in her salad bowl is pointed at her. I imagine she will soon launch in on having lived the wrong life for so long, and having suppressed her acting for so long. Whenever Lisa was that irritable I knew that she about to have her period and that she was living close to the crying threshold. The crying threshold was Lisa's coinage. I'd like to use it again now and ask Susanne directly: Are you close to your crying threshold? Presumably she'd appreciate such an accurate assessment of her situation. The waiter brings the chicken breast for Susanne and the focaccia for me, and we set upon our food all too hastily. But after a while Susanne would be in an even worse mood, because of course she would suspect that the crying threshold wasn't my invention. I would be intimidated and would admit that the idea was one of the few things I had left over from Lisa (aside from the money, which I wouldn't mention). Then I'd talk about how miserable it is that just when I'm halfway to the point where I understand one person, I can't help thinking about another person that I used to know *before*. I didn't realize how alike people are until late in life. For a long time I used to believe that they were all very different. Back then a crying threshold was only good as an idea put into words—but not the effect itself. It intruded on a lot of things Lisa might have told me, if the crying threshold hadn't impressed and distracted me the way it did. Crying threshold! I kept exclaiming, laughing as I did, so that I didn't even notice that Lisa was silenced by her own words, at least frequently.

I don't know anyone here, says Susanne, but I have the

feeling I just ate breakfast with them yesterday in some kind of communal kitchen.

I don't know what to say to that. I'm not sure I like the mood that's developing between Susanne and me. So to improve things I tell Susanne about a fantasy I had at the time I was writing her kitschy letters.

Back then I often imagined what it would be like if I came home one evening and you were sitting outside my door.

Would you have let me in?

It was just a fantasy.

So you wouldn't have let me in?

Of course I would have. Some evenings I was so sure of finding you outside my door that I was close to tears with excitement.

With excitement or expectation?

Back then I couldn't say.

We laugh.

Whenever I came close to tears I couldn't think, at least that's how it was back then.

Of course. And today?

Today I don't have any more fantasies.

Do you mean that?

Yes, at some point my fantasies all died off.

I don't believe you, says Susanne. They probably just grew on you in such a way that you no longer recognize them.

At this point the restaurant switches on the canned music—not a good sign for the further course of the evening. Susanne huffs and shoves the rest of her chicken towards the middle of the table. Presumably I should have made sure that we were in a restaurant without music. Susanne looks around. For a while we don't say anything to each other.

Look at those women, says Susanne. Just brimming with

contradictions! Sure their cleavage is sexy, but just look at how sad their faces are! Those eyes! Those bitter lips! You can tell that they're not getting much joy from their sexy cleavage.

I wonder about whether to order dessert, but then I ask: Should we leave?

Let's finish our wine, says Susanne.

A waiter has already noticed that we want to leave. He comes by and places the check on the edge of the table.

Would you spend the night at my place?

If you can stand having me, I say.

I wanted to ask you if you could stand me.

We laugh.

But there's a task you have to perform, says Susanne.

I wait.

Unfortunately I often wake up in the night, says Susanne, at least when I'm a little wound up or on edge. I'll frequently turn on the light and look at my sore tongue, I get panicky about cancer and ovaries and all that. There's half a chocolate bar on my nightstand, so if I talk too much you have to shove a little piece of chocolate in my mouth and then gently press my head into the pillow. Then I'll be able to fall back asleep with chocolate slowly melting in my mouth.

I accept the task.

In her bedroom Susanne asks if I like her outfit. She's wearing a stylized flight suit made of pale gray light natural fibers with diagonally placed zippers, which have been half open the entire evening. Beneath that is a luminous lemon-yellow blouse, cut to reveal a necklace with childishly small pearls. Susanne had applied a bit of gold dust under her eyes, which she now wipes off. She also removes her pyramid-shaped clip earrings.

I'm at a loss, I say truthfully, and then, to keep my answer from sounding too disappointing, I add: Generally speaking women overestimate the effect of their clothes, at least on men. Most men don't really care how a woman is dressed.

Are you one of those men?

I'm afraid I am.

She takes half a bar of chocolate from her nightstand and places it on the other side of the bed. Along with a box of matches. One by one she lights six candles that are standing in a tall candelabrum on top of a chest.

I often shop at this small boutique, and sometimes the owner has a blouse or a dress that she's worn two or three times herself and doesn't want to sell anymore, so she gives it to me.

Mmm, I say, distractedly.

I see you're really not interested in clothes at all.

Do I have to apologize for that?

Susanne laughs and moves the candelabrum a little further away. I catch sight of a small roll of aspirin on the bottom of a fruit bowl that's half-filled with oranges and apples and think to myself: Yes, of course.

Don't get it in your head that I'm all kitschy and want to be made love to by candlelight, says Susanne. The reason's simpler than that: I just don't want to be looked at too closely.

My God, I answer, that's something else women tend to overestimate.

I think you're just trying to reassure me, says Susanne.

And me.

At her core Susanne is presumably melancholic, which is why we can talk to each other and why we get along reasonably well. Although it's still not clear to me if she's aware of her own melancholy. The various material fetishes surrounding her (too many clothes, too much entertainment, too much search for meaning, too much decoration) would suggest she isn't.

You have to dare to be boring, I say.

Why?

It's impossible to deny that love is boring in the long run.

I can't afford to do that, says Susanne.

What's stopping you?

As it is I've been struggling half my life against the idea that I'm not even there.

Boring women go the farthest; their love is enduring and deep, I say.

Susanne sets two oranges and an apple next to the candelabrum.

Are you going to have an orange? I ask.

No, I just want a clear view of the fruit when I'm in bed, otherwise after a while I get the impression that I'm lying in a mortuary.

You think too much, I say.

Of course I do, says Susanne, don't you?

We laugh and kiss. Then she sits on the edge of the bed with her legs uncovered and asks: Can you look at me once with a critical eye?

I sit on the only chair in the room and examine Susanne. I'm a little afraid that a woman like Susanne wants her sex chic, just like the food and the restaurants and the clothes and the weekend.

Well? asks Susanne.

Well what?

Don't you notice anything?

I don't know what you're getting at.

Then look more closely.

I look at Susanne as acutely and observantly as I possibly can at a little after 11 p.m.

Don't you see, says Susanne, that my knees have a second pair growing in underneath?

I examine Susanne's knees without saying anything.

At first they were just indistinct lumps, says Susanne. I

thought that after a while they'd go away. Fat chance! They kept getting bigger and bigger and rounder and rounder and now it looks as if I have *two* knees on each leg. My legs look like an old woman's!

Susanne palpates her legs as if they were diseased body parts.

I take off my shirt and pants and say: There are only two real changes that happen as we get older—with men the ears get longer and with women it's the nose.

Susanne laughs and forgets about her double knees, at least for the moment. She pulls me down onto the bed and kisses me fiercely, as if she's racing against the clock. I'm surprised and at the same time I tell myself that I'm wrong to be surprised. The only thing that's happening here is what you set it in motion: you went and made yourself important for a woman. Susanne kisses me as she turns me on my back. She can't wait until I have enough of an erection to push inside her. She sits on top of my half-erect penis and then lays her upper body on mine. Maybe she's ashamed that her breasts are no longer firm. We've gotten off to a false start; we ought to be able to try again from the beginning. I enter her, but since I'm not yet hard enough I slip right back out. In the process I notice that I've forgotten to take off my socks. Right away it occurs to me that that's something Susanne won't be able to stand. At the moment it's impossible for me to pull them off inconspicuously and make them disappear. As far as I'm concerned the mishap doesn't spoil anything—on the contrary. Mishaps bring out our innocence; for me, they are a barely perceptible reminder of the fact that my knowledge of life is and always has been insufficient. I suddenly slide into my basic feeling that I've never been able to fully deal with life and that I am therefore living as if by mistake. Meanwhile Susanne's body is soft and fills me with childlike trust. But there's nothing to stop the feeling of living life by mistake, and it will soon lead to imagining a small, humiliating failure. That's another feeling I'm familiar with. I'm used to moving ahead in the midst of failure. For a while I don't know what will happen or how I'll get out of it, but I keep going—long enough, as it turns out, that I suddenly sense I'm in the middle of a second start, a new beginning. Now Susanne and I aren't saying anything. I lift her up and lay her down beside me. Meanwhile I've managed to wriggle my feet under a corner of the bedspread. Susanne's sex gives off a somewhat sour odor, which she probably objects to, but which makes me aroused. All of a sudden the bed smells like the breadbox in my mother's kitchen that was almost always open. Susanne looks at me; I'd really like to chase away her nervousness and say to her: Don't worry, you smell like a nice old bakery. Presumably she wouldn't approve of that image either. Our ardor demands grandeur and it's forbidden to diminish it with everyday notions. I turn around and open her legs as I slide my lower half out of the bed. Susanne sees what I'm up to, thrusts her abdomen in my direction, and spreads her legs as far as she can. I bend over her and kiss her sharp-smelling sex. That's the only way I can show her that I don't have anything against the bready smell of love—on the contrary. Susanne whimpers quietly and holds my head with both hands. I purse my lips into a point and suck her labia into my mouth and let them rub against my lower teeth as they slide out. And right then I think of Himmelsbach. I see him and Margot walking through the city. It seems as if my lovemaking with Susanne is disturbed a second time. I scoff at Himmelsbach and his adolescent advances. I let Susanne's labia glide out of my mouth and think: You see, Himmelsbach, that's how it's done. I kiss Susanne's sex longer than I intended—the extra time is to drive Himmelsbach from my consciousness. But I don't know if it's working, and so my neck and head break out in a sweat. If it goes on like this Susanne and I will need a third attempt.

I don't know what I should do to stop thinking about Himmelsbach. All that's left for me to do is continue my engrossment in Susanne's sex, and even that seems to be fading by the moment. I have this feeling that I'm always making little bows to life. And at the same time, what I am bowing is life itself. The hope arises between Susanne's legs that one day, when I have made enough bows to it, I will be able to authorize my life. Ultimately it should no longer be clear whether I'm bowing to life or life has bowed on its own. Then my unbelievable forbearance will finally triumph. Evidently my bowing idea is working. Himmelsbach vanishes from my thoughts; I've stopped talking to him. Perhaps it's also the bready smell of Susanne's arousal that makes my penis hard again. I get up and move Susanne's body a little closer to the middle of the bed. This time she keeps still, so I can enter her without complications. Jubilation that comes on the heels of a near failure is always the strongest. My thrusts are like completed bows, now to love as well. Susanne is now squeaking like a small animal. It's as if she'll never want to say real words again. But no less than two minutes later she tells me that I have to be careful.

What should I do, I ask, do I have to pull out?

Stay as long as you can and then come on my stomach.

Her request arouses my imagination so that I can no longer extend our intercourse. Susanne turns her face to the side and holds out her arms. Luckily I'm not one of those men whose semen escapes without internal notification. I can feel the moment when an ejaculation is forming and when it's on the verge of release. At that point I break off from Susanne and then bend quickly over her; the semen pours onto her stomach. Susanne sighs and swallows and helps me down off of her. A little later she starts smearing my semen on her stomach with her hand. I watch her a while and want to ask something, but then it occurs to me that when a woman has grown still, it's best not to ask what she is doing.

110

# 10

----

I'VE SPENT THE WHOLE DAY WONDERING IF I SHOULD GIVE in to my anger and give up my work as a shoe tester. It's almost evening by the time I decide to keep the job, at least for now, despite the pay cut. At the moment I'm sitting in my room typing out the test reports for the shoes I recently received from Habedank. Of course I've been lax on occasion before, but this is the first time I've completely fabricated my evaluations. From now on I'll deliver nothing but made-up reports and then sell the shoes at the flea market to compensate for the decrease in pay. It's been raining for days. I sit in my front room next to an open window. I appreciate the smell that issues from the depths of the city after a long rain—a mix of mortar, mud, mold, urine, dust, marsh, rust. Now and then I interrupt my work, stroll around the apartment and observe the people in the buildings opposite. They, too, observe me: we don't hide from one another, and occasionally we acknowledge each other with a quick smile. Maybe the rain has made us mellow. At present the most noteworthy person is a woman about sixty years old who carefully sweeps the dirt and dust on her balcony into a small pile. But then she leaves the pile where it is and goes inside her apartment, and occasionally glances at the pile from there. As far as I'm concerned there's no need for anything weightier than that. A wind comes up and scatters the little pile. The woman watches the destruction of her work, but does nothing to stop it. On the third rainy day Frau Balkhausen calls. For a moment I'm a little taken aback and as a result I don't say very much. The truth is that I don't really know what might tie me to Frau Balkhausen—a fact I evidently can't completely conceal. I'm soon overcome by my most common phone sensation: namely, that I really ought to be bracing myself for bad news, but I've started preparing too late, so I'll have to take the blow without any protection. As it turns out, Frau Balkhausen doesn't deliver more than a caricature of bad news, anyway. She's one of those people who can converse with me without my participation.

I've just had three things conk out on me, she says. My bathroom light went kaput, a vase broke, and I tore the hem of my blue pants.

Frau Balkhausen laughs; I say nothing or actually I start a short sentence that never gets off the ground.

So then I decided to give you a call! says Frau Balkhausen. After all, you said I should! I am speaking with the Institute for Memory Arts, am I not?

My God! I had forgotten both the Institute and Frau Balkhausen. I start to laugh but I can see that laughing won't be enough to make the Institute go away.

I've thought about your Institute a lot! says Frau Balkhausen.

We spend far too long talking about whether we should meet in the mid-afternoon, the late afternoon, or the evening. Now I remember that Frau Balkhausen had wanted to book a single Experience Session with the Institute for Memory Arts—that is to say with me. She'd prefer to meet in the afternoon.

In the evening we'd have to sit in a restaurant, she says, but then we'd be together with all those awful experience proletarians. I don't want to have anything more to do with them!

I've never heard of experience proletarians, I wonder what they could be or whether Frau Balkhausen just invented the phrase to show me she's a discriminating and difficult person who isn't satisfied with ready-made experiences. Throughout the conversation I keep glancing into my open leaf room. By now the leaves have completely dried out and either rolled or crinkled themselves into impressive shapes.

At once I see why I longed to have a leaf room: I ought to have at least one place in the world where nothing can get too close to me, where I'm not subject to any demands. When I walk among the leaves I even lose the feeling that there's something I need to account for. The leaf room is unquestionably the invention of my soul, which is very possibly quite cunning.

I'm looking for something unique, says Frau Balkhausen, a genuine, personal experience. You understand what I'm saying, right?

Although I don't have the slightest idea what I'm supposed to do with Frau Balkhausen, I arrange to meet her at 4 p.m.

At the pier.

At the pier, Frau Balkhausen repeats, and we hang up.

In fact the summer is coming to an end, which is of far more interest to me. The grass is losing its sheen, and the leaves are not only turning yellow, they are also beginning to fall. For days a few seagulls have been circling over the roofs. Where do they come from? Perhaps they were enticed by the rain, lured into thinking there's a large body of water somewhere nearby. Now they watch the housewives from high in the air as the women hang fresh laundry in their balcony niches far below. Every day doors open up onto balconies all around town, women step outside, and feel whether the laundry is dry, half-dry or just about dry. As I observe an elderly lady who is just now carrying a plastic basket full of freshly washed clothes onto her balcony, I deduce that doing laundry has made her slightly insane. She hangs up her clothes and disappears back inside her apartment. Not more than two minutes later she feels the clothes for the first time to see if they aren't dry. She returns inside, but then quickly reappears on the balcony, where she repeats her inspection. In the end she allows her own insane impatience to drive her to exhaustion. Or perhaps it's the other way around—maybe the exhaustion gives her a momentary respite from her insanity. In a short period she touches the clothes ten to fifteen times, then suddenly collapses into a wicker armchair, where she stays seated among the bed sheets, which are gently fluttering back and forth. She watches another neighbor, who has stepped onto her own balcony just to smoke, and falls asleep. Now her head is resting against the rear wall of the balcony, her mouth is open, her hands lie motionless in her lap. The sheets hanging to her right and left look like winding-sheets soon to be wrapped around her body. But then the woman wakes up again and immediately feels the laundry, which still isn't dry. What a fantastic picture: the dead woman awakes and wards off her real death by touching her own winding-sheets. Meanwhile the smoker has already lit her second cigarette. Being watched has made her a little angry and aggressive. She looks around with flickering, melancholy eyes and takes too hard a drag on her cigarette. A moment later I find myself ensnared in my own insanity. On the way to the toilet I spend too much time gazing at the hall mirror and suddenly I'm convinced that my face has reverted to that of an eleven-year-old-boy—whitish, round, and moonlike, edged with blond hair. The eyes are blue and watery, the lips stick dryly together, the skin is a little rough, the mouth has a stale taste that won't go away, the scalp is constantly itching, the tongue refuses to move—only the small moon eyes dart back and forth, always asking: When does the suffering begin in life? And what makes it start? Will someone make fun of me? Will another child soon say to me, *you dimwit?* And then grab my ridiculous sweater and in the end make fun of me because of my clothes? And will I then go home and sit down on a couch, just like now, and wait for the horror to pass? I can't let Frau Balkhausen see me with *this* face. My childhood keeps coursing through me with all its flitting and fleeting this way and that and with all its failures and fears, pinning me onto the sofa for nearly an hour. Then I get up and open the door to the armoire. Now there are at least two strange sights in the room: an open armoire and myself. Just like the woman on the balcony, I stick my hand into the laundry that was last ironed by Lisa. I take out a tea towel and carry it around the apartment for a while. I get tired like the woman on the balcony. I lie back down on the sofa, using the folded tea towel as a pillow. Lisa's smell comes wafting from the tea towel; it helps me fall asleep. I sleep for about an hour. Then the specter of the child's face is gone.

The daylong rains have caused the river to overflow its banks. The broad meadows by the river are mostly flooded. The pier has been retracted; the river is pushing and thrusting and coursing along the stone embankment. Frau Balkhausen is standing near a fire engine watching a few men as they seal off basement windows with sandbags. She's wearing an earth-toned dress and appears resigned. She looks off to the side, intimidated and a little pained, as I walk up to her and say hello. We had intended to go for a walk, but then we discover that we both enjoy the sight of the river as it surges past. So we sit down on a bench and watch the earthy-yellow water. A moment later Frau Balkhausen addresses the problem of her boredom.

No matter what I do, she says, I always know in advance that I'll soon be bored to death. In recent months it's gotten so bad I thought I should do something about it . . . and then I met you, as if through some providence.

I give a start but Frau Balkhausen doesn't notice.

What kind of boredom are you suffering from? I ask. Acute individual boredom or is it more like mass boredom?

Acute boredom? asks Frau Balkhausen.

Do you have the feeling, I ask, whenever you're by yourself, that the boredom originates somewhere inside of you, that you can't protect yourself against it, that it simply comes, so to speak, with malicious suddenness?

115

Yes, exactly, with malicious suddenness.

That would be acute individual boredom, I say. Or is it like this: You're with other people, in the theater or the swimming pool or somewhere, you're enjoying yourself, you've made a special point of going to the theater or the swimming pool because you wanted to enjoy yourself, but all of a sudden you sense that everything that you're enjoying actually bores you.

That happens just as often! says Frau Balkhausen. And then it's particularly embarrassing. I'll be with a whole group of friends, convinced that I'm having a good time, that I'm feeling good, and all of a sudden I sense that nothing really grabs me anymore, that everything is going right by me—it's really a horrible feeling. Is that mass boredom or acute individual boredom?

Now we're in the middle of a proper therapeutic conversation; I can't stop myself any more than I can stop Frau Balkhausen.

What was your last attack like? Which came first—your own boredom or that of the others?

My last attack . . . hmm . . . let's see, says Frau Balkhausen. Oh, right . . . my God . . . Tübingen . . . that was terrible . . . I'm embarrassed to talk about it.

Were you alone? I ask, wiping the sweat of embarrassment off my brow. Frau Balkhausen is watching me, but I believe she thinks my perspiration is a sign of my seriousness and absorption in her problem.

No, says Frau Balkhausen, I went with my boyfriend. He'd read an article about a large Impressionist exhibit in the Tübingen Kunsthalle. My immediate response was: Let's go! Impressionists! My God! We can finally see the originals. We were so happy about it. We planned to spend the night so we could look at the pictures a second time the following day. After all, you can't see all there is to see with famous paintings like that in just one viewing, right? But

116

then, after driving for hours, we reach Tübingen and walk into the Kunsthalle. Just off to the right is this picture . . . um . . . it's called *Harvest* or something like that, it doesn't matter, this wonderful summer picture, I'm sure you know it! All of a sudden I feel stricken by this horrible boredom! Good God, I thought, Cézanne. I look over to the left, and there's another summer picture, I can't recall the title off-hand, and I thought: You know, today these pictures are hanging in every classroom and every office—they're impossible to look at anymore! Run-of-the-mill waiting-room art! The boredom just paralyzed me. I could hardly take another step. Then I looked at my boyfriend; his mind was already somewhere else. He'd started to get bored on the drive down. He just hadn't said anything so as not to spoil my fun. And then he told me that on the autobahn he'd been imagining the crowd in front of the pictures, being jostled from all sides, a guided tour on your left for housewives from Reutlingen, one on your right for housewives from Böblingen, behind you the smell of old men sweating, and in front of you a field trip from Ravensburg full of rambunctious school kids! After that we got in the car and drove back home.

Without having seen the pictures?

Yes, says Frau Balkhausen, without having seen the pictures.

Frau Balkhausen is half-exhausted and half-distressed by her story. We say nothing and watch the water flowing by. A small wooden table drifts past, upside-down. I wonder why Frau Balkhausen told me the story of her Tübingen boredom. I can only find one explanation: Frau Balkhausen is a roaming incapacitator. I'm powerless against her. A saturated mattress floats by, followed by some branches and brambles that have snapped or been torn off. A police car stops at the bridge. Three policemen jump out and start closing off the entrance. The stairs up to the bridge are under water;

the bridge itself has become impassable. I'm happy that there's something going on for us to watch, since I have no idea what I should ask next or how I should analyze Frau Balkhausen's account or how I should advise her in her need. At the same time, I conclude that no one can/could withstand Frau Balkhausen's juggernaut. Nor does she really want anyone to help her; she just wants someone to incapacitate, and today it's me. For that reason I could conceivably admit to her that our meeting is a misunderstanding. Frau Balkhausen, I am not an experience therapist, I was just joking around, and unfortunately you were taken in. Most likely Frau Balkhausen would have to laugh at that, because I still assumed that *she* had been taken in by *me*. A TV van pulls up to the bridge. A cameraman, a soundman and a reporter climb out, along with an assistant who unpacks the equipment. Frau Balkhausen and I watch, time passes pleasantly, my unmasking as a swindler and a charlatan is again postponed. Meanwhile I practice what I'm going to say in my excuse. It was just the champagne speaking. My temperament sometimes gets the better of me. Do you know how often my big mouth has gotten me in trouble? Something like that ought to do it. The reporter takes her microphone and asks passersby why they are here and what they find interesting about the flood. The passersby give evasive or embarrassed answers. They say *just because* or *happened to be* or *I don't know* or else they just go *ummm*.

Once again no one is asking me, says Frau Balkhausen next to me.

Would you like to be asked? How would you answer?

Of course I'm embarrassed too, says Frau Balkhausen, but if I weren't embarrassed, I'd say that I love floods because I like watching the world go under.

Frau Balkhausen laughs, I laugh with her.

You absolutely have to say that sentence into the camera, I say.

But I'm embarrassed, she says. When the camera is pointed at me I won't get a word out, and besides they wouldn't broadcast my answer anyway.

I don't believe that, I say, on the contrary, these days they only broadcast what's shocking or unusual.

But I'm still embarrassed, says Frau Balkhausen.

Why?

The truth is I'd really prefer to say something absolutely proper, I don't want to stick out.

I don't believe you.

You mean you think I want to stick out?

Yes.

And how should I go about it?

I'll go with you.

And then?

We'll walk over to the reporter very casually, I say. The reporter will notice you and hold out the microphone and then you'll say exactly what you just told me.

Frau Balkhausen resists a little, but she's also excited by the possibility that she might actually get to speak on camera. We stand up and act as if we wanted to leave, but then we turn around and walk towards the TV team. The reporter breaks away from her team and goes up to Frau Balkhausen; her face is friendly. Then it happens exactly as I said it would. And Frau Balkhausen finds the strength to say her sentence: I like floods because I like watching the world go under.

The reporter is pleasantly surprised and says: How original!! Then she adds: But the world isn't going under at all, is it?!

Of course not, says Frau Balkhausen, it only looks that way, see what I mean?

Aha, says the reporter, so you're into appearances?

Yes, says Frau Balkhausen, appearances and as-ifs! You think all this junk is finally floating away, but it turns out it's

119

still there, or else it's coming right back! Just a little flood and nothing more!

The reporter laughs for a second and then lowers her microphone. That's a nice statement, she says.

Will you broadcast it? asks Frau Balkhausen.

I can't say for certain, but I think so.

When?

Today at 7 on the evening news.

The reporter thanks Frau Balkhausen and wanders off to interview other flood-tourists. Frau Balkhausen is so enthusiastic that she puts her arm in mine.

It's unbelievable, Frau Balkhausen says as we're walking away. I actually said exactly what I think—I don't believe I've ever done that.

The two-hour experience session she had booked is over. Frau Balkhausen opens her small purse and hands me the two hundred marks we had agreed on. I don't know if she notices the various inhibitions that pass through me right then. I struggle to keep any second thoughts at bay, but in vain. An embarrassing discomfort descends on me. Then Frau Balkhausen says goodbye.

May I call you again some time? she asks.

Of course, I say, with inane eagerness, and throw in a nod.

Frau Balkhausen heads off to the left towards the South Bridge, which is still passable. More and more rubberneckers stop at the pier, which is now almost completely submerged. Now the footbridge is entirely under water except for the iron railing. Presumably Frau Balkhausen would like the sight of the unmoored railing rocking back and forth. The police finish cordoning off the bridge. The TV team stows their gear in their van. The suddenly vacated riverbank captivates me. I especially like a wooden rowboat that's tied off to a tree, swinging loosely back and forth in the current. The hull is half full of water; the boat doesn't rise com-

pletely to the surface but neither does it sink. I instantly
think: That's exactly how I feel. But just as instantly the idea
of equating my life with the boat strikes me as absurd. Good
God, this compulsion to see things meaningfully is really
getting on my nerves. I can almost hear my own voice
admonishing me: A boat is a boat is a boat. Right then a
duck swims by, with one leg sticking up in an odd way. And
although I just admonished myself to stop seeing things
meaningfully, this sentence does occur to me: Good God,
now even the ducks are disabled. A few seconds later the
duck pulls its leg back into the water and goes on paddling
normally. I wait a while longer, to give Frau Balkhausen a
good head start, then I, too, vanish in the direction of the
South Bridge. If I wanted to express the peculiarity of life at
this moment I'd have to toss my jacket into the brown flood-
water. I'd wait until I was on the South Bridge, and then I'd
fling the jacket in a high arc into the river. The jacket would
drift in the water; the current would slurp and slop all
around it, and then those words would become the latest
words for the peculiarity of life: slurping and slopping. A little later I really do step onto the South Bridge. Immediately
I feel tempted to throw my jacket over the railing. I don't
know why I don't. If I could observe the jacket from above
(it would soon be totally soaked so that only I could tell it
was *my* jacket), watch it drifting downriver, eddying around
in the process, then I might be able to understand the
strangeness of the fact that I just earned two hundred marks
thanks to a ridiculous misunderstanding and an equally
ridiculous chat. But I keep my jacket on, I get over the peculiarity of the past two hours, and I arrive at the other end of
the bridge. The only thing I feel is a kind of compassion for
my death, which is hopefully still far off. Heavens—another
sentence laden with meaning! The truth is, I am only experiencing my interest in our common trivial fate: at the end
of my life is death, there's nothing further. I even know why

I didn't throw my jacket into the water: despite all the peculiarity I have yet to go insane. The fear of insanity was always just the fear of giving up. I turn onto Chamisso Strasse, which is very busy. Benevolently I observe the bustle of the people. But then I can't avoid a terrible sight: Himmelsbach is pushing a small shopping cart piled high with brochures. He stops in front of each apartment building and shoves a few brochures underneath the door. A terrible thought occurs to me: Himmelsbach is failing in my stead. From the beginning, ever since I witnessed his Paris debacle, it has been his task to show me the mirror image of a failing man, in order to protect me from myself. I am powerless; a gigantic chaos swirls through me, bringing tears to my eyes. I slow down and hide behind parked cars. I don't want to run into Himmelsbach and don't want to speak with him. He wouldn't understand about the two of us, and I wouldn't have the strength or the skill to explain my distress. It's becoming clearer by the moment that my tears were only meant for Himmelsbach at first and that now they're meant for me alone. I, too, would be delivering idiotic brochures throughout the city, if I could no longer do anything else. My greatest fear was always that I might someday have to show my enormous pliability in public. Fortunately something silly is happening once again. And once again it's Himmelsbach who frees me from the dismay that's half meant for him and half for myself. He's bending over for the second time to comb his hair in some car's sideview mirror. Himmelsbach, I mutter at him good-naturedly, you even want to make a good impression on your own sad plight. My compassion doesn't want to play along. I step into a dusty dry boutique and wait until the air conditioning starts to dry my tears.

# 11

LATE ONE WEDNESDAY MORNING I GATHER ALL THE LEAVES
I had spread out in Lisa's former room. Soon Susanne will
be going in and out of my apartment, and I don't feel any
need to talk about past frustrations with her (or anyone else).
Some of the leaves had housed tiny black beetles, no bigger
than a pinhead, which over time slipped from their perches
and perished in the artificial fibers of the carpet—though I
have found at least two of the creatures still alive. Gripped
by a mild panic that causes me to retrieve the vacuum cleaner from the closet, I start by cleaning Lisa's room, then the
hall, and then the other rooms. I believe it's the first time
I've cleaned the apartment this thoroughly since Lisa left. It
takes me nearly an hour to finish. Afterwards I collapse onto
a chair, sweating, drained, and blank. After about fifteen
minutes an image emerges from the middle of the blank-
ness—the recollection of a childhood amusement at least as
old as that of walking among the fallen leaves. A moving
sequence unfolds before me or rather inside me, centering
on an open coal truck. The vehicle turns onto the street
where I lived with my parents and stops in front of one of
the apartment buildings. It's an old rickety flatbed truck with
a simple tailgate, probably an Opel Blitz or a pre-war
Hanomag. The driver backs up against the side of the building, then he and his co-worker hop out of the cab and open
the tailgate. The two men are black from the coal-dust.
Having donned cowl-like caps that are even blacker than
they are, they begin carrying the heavy sacks filled with bri-
quettes, coke, or egg-coal off the truck and into the basement. The men make a few attempts to dump the coal
through an open window at street level directly into the

basement—without great success. Much of the coal simply hits the wall and winds up on the sidewalk, forming a gigantic cloud of coal dust. At that point I—as a fourteen-year-old—turn the corner and then spend far too long watching the spectacle. I soon conclude that the spilled coal facing me is early proof of the impossibility of life, though at the same time I'm happy about the growing mess. I watch the coal men until they're finished with their work, and look forward to what's coming next. An inept housewife steps outside, armed with a broom, and tries to sweep away the grime. She can't do this without again whipping up the dust, though I have to concede that the sweeping does lessen the actual amount, albeit very slowly. For at least ten minutes the sweeping housewife moves like a tireless phantom in the dust she stirred up—reinforcing my sense of life's impossibility. At the same time I'm fascinated by the way the dust gets into the woman's hair and clothes. I feel an unfamiliar, inexplicable pleasure. In only half the time my transforming eye converted one of life's momentary dust-ups into a generally dusty life: I simply couldn't understand why most people put up with it the way they did. I can no longer remember if I had already resolved not to give in so easily to all of life's dustiness. At least not without a long, drawn-out authorization proceeding, which is still going on today, but will presumably be over soon, if my instinct isn't leading me astray. It never occurred to me until just this moment that that may have been the first time I fell victim to this meaningful seeing of things. Right now I'd like to see a coal truck turn the corner. I stand at the window in Lisa's former room in a wistful daze and look down at the street. Right then the phone rings. A woman is on the line who introduces herself as Frau Tschackert.

I got your number from Frau Balkhausen, she's a colleague of mine from work.

Ah-ha.

She was telling me about a wonderful experience session she had with a gentleman from your Institute.

Ah, yes, I say.

I was wondering, says Frau Tschackert, if I might also be able to, um, book an afternoon like that with your Institute.

How, um, great, I say.

Frau Balkhausen is thrilled. I'm sure she'll call on you again, says Frau Tschackert. Imagine, yesterday evening she saw herself on TV for the first time, and that was thanks to you, she told me.

That's wonderful, I say.

Isn't it! exclaims Frau Tschackert.

I probably ought to end the conversation now. But despite my rising embarrassment, I "schedule" Frau Tschackert "an appointment" for next week, in the late afternoon, shortly after work, two hours for two hundred marks "as usual." Frau Tschackert is happy, we finish our conversation.

Right after that I want to think some more about whether seeing that coal truck as a child was the first time I practiced some elaborate deception on myself, but I can no longer recover the trail of memories that leads to the old images. Some time later a brief storm comes rushing in over the rooftops, making me think of one of my mother's sayings: Lightning makes the milk go sour. If Lisa were here she'd say: Now that's a real summer storm! It doesn't cool anything off at all! It occurs to me that I haven't seen or spoken to Lisa in several weeks. It's as if she had stepped out of my life forever. I instantly correct myself: it doesn't just seem that way—she *has* stepped out of my life. I'm even somewhat glad I haven't run into her these past few days. Presumably I wouldn't have been able to resist the temptation to do a bit of gloating. Can you imagine, I'm running an Institute that doesn't exist and making money in the process—quite the modern life! Just think, I sometimes say important things, even though I never wanted to be important myself. And: I'm seeing someone again! And most unheard-of of all: If all goes well I'll be earning a regular paycheck at the Gazette! Seeing how astonished Lisa would be to hear all that, I would tack on a few even more pompous announcements. By the way, my existential dilemma is fading away, don't you think? I no longer have the desire to scrutinize myself. I'm no longer waiting for the outside world to finally fit my inner texts! I've stopped being the blind passenger of my own life!

I'm happy I don't have to say these sentences. Finally Lisa slips back out of my thoughts. Survival is followed by a peculiar kind of stillness. Suddenly everything is peaceful, as if there'd never been a struggle. I look around the apartment; not far from me is an outdated newspaper. Instead of the headline POVERTY ACT REVEALED IN DISTRICT PARLIAMENT I read POVERTY ACT REVELED IN DISTRICT PARLIAMENT. Even though I've never seen a district parliament from the inside, for a moment I'm delighted that the lawmakers are finally reveling in poverty. The storm has passed; the grass is gleaming on the little lawns in front of the apartment houses. It's still summer; the windows are open everywhere. My birthday is in two weeks. I had forgotten about it or rather had skipped over it, as I've done before on many other occasions, but Susanne has known my birthday since childhood and wants to celebrate it. I think about Frau Tschackert, whom I don't know at all. I don't have the faintest idea what I'll do with her. Today is the Summerfest, which I'll be attending for the Gazette so I can write a *breezy* (that's Messerschmidt's word) article. I casually asked Susanne if she wanted to go with me to the Summerfest. Even more casually I mentioned that I was covering it for the Gazette. Susanne didn't react, which led me to conclude that my casualness came off all right. I consider confessing to Susanne tonight that I'm making money off a Swindle-

Institute I invented as a joke. Presumably that will make Susanne laugh, and the Institute will be forgotten.

A little later I take the three plastic bags of leaves and go outside. I don't want anyone watching me dump leaves out of plastic bags. I find a little, out-of-the-way park and step in between two bushes as tall as a man. I empty the bags right between the bushes. Now I'll check Lisa's, or rather my, account. I haven't gone back to the small branch office since my first attempt at withdrawing money failed. On my way I stop at a bakery on Dominikaner Strasse and buy a fresh loaf of white bread. The bread is still warm; it reminds me of Lisa's and Susanne's bodies both at once. For a moment I'm confused, but then I accept the simultaneity. I clamp the bread under my arm, keeping the smell of both women as close to me as possible. Inside the bank I see new faces and new details. A very young teller, whom I've never seen before, watches me as I fill out a withdrawal form. I pass her the paper along with my account card. The teller checks both form and card while I examine the statements for the past several weeks. It's like I thought: as a kind of compensation for leaving me (I'm sticking fast to this version), Lisa is letting me have the money in the account—or more precisely, the unspent remnants of her pension from the past two years. The teller has verified that my signature and card are both genuine and that I am entitled to withdraw money from Lisa's account. I stash the money in my wallet with a hint of shame, which my body has known since childhood. Outside on the street I can no longer keep myself from breaking off a corner of the bread. I bore a hole in the loaf with my finger and start sticking tiny pieces of the dough into my mouth as I walk.

The honey-colored sky doesn't change color until evening. Susanne is wearing a simply cut light gray chintz dress with open shoulders and a half-open back. A black and red scarf is waving around her neck. No jewelry, no earrings,

127

not even a bracelet. She is subtly made-up and in a good mood. The high point of the Summerfest will be a laser show on the market square. Susanne has never seen a laser show. I haven't either, which I don't admit to her. Nor do I tell her that I've never wanted to see one. I assume that my actively felt ambivalence makes me more progressively modern than the average Summerfest attendee. For a while Susanne and I are dumbstruck by the enormous lighting fixtures, which are mounted on the bed of a truck in the middle of the market square. In one or two hours bright beams of light will be fired off into the heavens from right here. The square is full of stands and booths selling champagne, pretzels, and grilled food. An open-air movie theater has been set up on the left, where HILARIOUS CARTOONS will be shown ALL NIGHT LONG. At the opposite end is a LIVE STAGE, where THE WAVES will be playing later on. One of the organizers picks up a microphone and calls the whole area the PARTY MILE. More and more people are coming from the side streets and spreading out around the square. Presumably they are the ones Frau Balkhausen described as experience proletarians. I look at the people and I don't look at them. I know them and I don't know them. They interest me and they don't interest me. I already know too much about them and I still don't know enough. Susanne regards the suntanned waiters, each of whom looks as if he kept a yacht on the Mediterranean that he's just renting out at the moment. They walk carefully so as not to dirty their white aprons, which almost come down to the ground. Young people laugh with their faces, older people with their bodies. If the world could still be criticized, I would probably have to find out now who is betraying, using, deceiving, exploiting whom. But Messerschmidt only wants a breezy article. Another organizer refers to the square as the FUN ZONE. Two tattooed men in undershirts and ragged pants take turns emptying a bottle of orange juice. They're wearing earrings and nose rings and have smoothly shaved scalps. Their arms are as thick as the plastic orange juice bottle. Roaming around and about with half-filled glasses is evidently a radical experience. It's palpably obvious that most of the fairgoers mistake this artificial life for the real thing. A woman passes Susanne and me while yelling in her companion's ear: I don't like it when my life turns into an investigation of my life. Another woman says: I didn't have any youth at all, don't you realize that? One man describes himself as a monogamous idealist and bites into a bratwurst. Another man says gently to the woman accompanying him: You're lucky you know me. Susanne looks at me and shrugs her shoulders. Slowly the evening twilight descends. THE WAVES step onstage and tune their instruments. A Tom-and-Jerry movie is playing in the open-air theater. I make countless observations and snip out the ones that aren't *breezy*. Presumably tonight I am joining the great team of world cosmetologists. The admonition follows at once: Good God, but you wanted to get away from these pretentious perceptions. People just want to concentrate on what they consider shocking, there's nothing more to it. Everybody is doing what he can to create a feeling of belonging to the world. Susanne brings two glasses of champagne. To find shelter from the roar of THE WAVES, we lean against the back wall of a steak stand. Susanne and I talk about how amazed we are that the entertainments of a given time are always such a good match for the people of that particular era.

Why weren't there any laser shows in the fifties? asks Susanne.

Because in the fifties a laser show would have reminded everyone too much of the war and all the flak, I answer.

What's flak? asks Susanne.

Flak is anti-aircraft artillery, I say; during the war they used huge spotlights to search for enemy aircraft.

That sounds like a decent explanation, says Susanne, but I still don't believe it.

Do you have another one?

During the fifties there wasn't any need for a laser show because boredom hadn't achieved the world domination it has today, says Susanne.

We laugh and drink. I can't resist watching a woman whose blouse is emblazoned with the words HARMONY SYMPHONY MEMORY. The hand-sized letters spelled out across the woman's blouse are made of overlapping stitched sequins that shimmer and rattle softly whenever the woman moves. The head of the Cultural Events Office steps onto the lighting platform. I'm very happy, he says, that our city is putting on its first ever SPECTACLE OF LIGHT. Applause. A total of fifteen spotlights have been set up, each with a range of forty kilometers. Applause. Tonight they will consume a total of approximately half a million kilowatts. Applause. Nearly one hundred special lamps and a dozen different lighting systems have been erected. Applause. I take notes. Susanne holds my champagne glass and watches me. The anxiety over my almost-failed life metamorphoses into excitement about my newly-discovered way out. At the same time I can't quite fully identify with people's happiness and expectations. I'm convinced that all these happy people will become merciless at the first opportunity, if mercilessness suddenly looks profitable. I myself am embroiled in this nasty work or in this work of nastiness or in the nastiness of the real—at the moment I can't really tell one from the other. I'm flinching at the work and now I think I might phone Messerschmidt tomorrow and turn down his offer. Isn't there a slope here somewhere with a lot of debris, where I can toss my jacket? But there's nothing except carnival booths, snack stands, and kiosks; I'll just have to go on carrying the feeling of debris inside me. Suddenly I notice a boy of about twelve who is constructing a lair on his balcony.

He's stretched a rope between the iron railing and two clothesline hooks, and is draping a wool blanket over the rope. He fastens the blanket with clothespins, and checks them from time to time to see how they are holding. He goes back inside the apartment several times and returns with additional wool blankets, towels and pillows. In between trips he glances below at the crowd milling about in the market square. The balcony is on the fourth floor of a simple tenement. I point out the boy and his lair to Susanne. I'm not sure if she realizes that the boy is rescuing my intentions. I don't understand anything about angels, nor do I believe in them, but I still consider it possible that this boy is whizzing between heaven and earth solely for my sake. He permits me to escape the confusion of work and time; he makes me escapable in the middle of an inescapable event. Now he's putting the roof on his lair. He attaches another clothesline between the balcony railing and the rolling shutter fixture at shoulder-height on the inside wall of the balcony. He draws the line taut, then tosses the last wool blanket he brought outside and fastens it on both ends with clothespins. The lair opens onto the balcony door. Behind that is presumably the kitchen, which is unlit. All of the apartment windows are unlit. The boy's parents are probably romping around the market square. The lair is set up so that two wool blankets meet along the railing. Now and then the boy shoves his hand between the edges of the blankets and opens them to form an observation slit. Barely discernible from below, the child's white hand and his motionless face appear between the wool blankets, for a few indescribable moments that rightly belong to the angels, if there are such things as angels. The boy vanishes for a while inside the apartment. The people in the open-air theater keep turning around in search of other scenes with greater or more extreme thrills. The head of the Cultural Events Office climbs down from the light stage. Shortly after that the first beams flare up and sweep across the firmament. THE WAVES hammer out a rhythm above the square. The boy reappears on the balcony, equipped with provisions and a bottle of mineral water for his lair. Evidently he's settling in for a longer stay. Susanne and I wander around and about a little, then we leave the Summerfest. Susanne is tired and slightly drunk. She wants to go to bed right away and sleep. I take her home and then go back to the market square one more time, just to get a longer look at the boy's lair. Once he opens his observation slit a handbreadth and surveys the noisy, surging masses for an extended period. His gaze is mistrustful, from a safe vantage—much like my own. After a little more than an hour I, too, head home and go to bed. At noon the next day I set off for the Gazette and drop off a breezy article for Messerschmidt. I walk across the market square since I want to see what has become of the lair. It's still there. I look up for a while, but there's no sign of the boy; presumably he's in school. A few minutes later a woman—probably his mother—steps out onto the balcony. She takes a plastic bucket inside, moving so as not to disturb the lair. Nothing is left of yesterday's fest. The laser show, the stage for THE WAVES, the open-air theater, the loud-speakers, the booths—all gone.